Robin

D1270079

the mukhtar's children

books by sally watson

THE MUKHTAR'S CHILDREN
THE HORNET'S NEST
OTHER SANDALS
LARK
TO BUILD A LAND
MISTRESS MALAPERT
HIGHLAND REBEL

the mukhtar's children

by sally watson

holt, rinehart and winston
new york   chicago   san francisco

for my delightful god-daughter karla

contents

1. the Black Goat

"Devil!" said Khalil earnestly. "Evil one! Son of *Shaitan!*" He made a grab and missed.

Quite possibly the black goat was indeed the son of Satan. It seemed highly likely. Almost certainly there was no other in the whole of Palestine that could compare in size or wickedness. Lowering sharp horns, he aimed himself threateningly at Khalil's midsection and charged.

Khalil, who knew very well how it felt to be butted, at once hurled himself sideways in a brilliant combination of dive, roll, and somersault.

"Look out, Yusif!" he yelled, quite unnecessarily.

When he looked up, *khaffiya* hanging rakishly over one ear, it was to see his small half brother and the goat circling each other in what looked like an old Arab folk dance. It was no such thing, of course. Each was merely trying to decide whether to attack or run.

"*Wallah!*" bleated Yusif, and "Bah!" jeered the goat, skipping nimbly to one side and heading up the hill. The last time he had gone right over the top, down into the next valley, and created havoc among the flocks of the Lebanese village down there. Today could be even worse, for his best friend Selim was ill with the bowel-sickness, and Buazza the dog was home with a poisoned paw, and Yusif was not much help.

"*Kus emmek!*" swore Khalil. "*Maskin!* Offspring of a thousand *djinn!*" After which he added several even more pungent expressions picked up lately from Uncle Kebab, which Yusif—deeply admiring—at once committed to memory. Even the black goat seemed impressed, for he glanced back with evil yellow eyes and suddenly began to dawdle. He nibbled some of the lush grass, already turning brown in the May heat. He had a bite of scarlet poppies, chewed them thoughtfully, and then tried some of the wild anemone that starred the hillside. Elaborately pretending not to see the two robed figures stalking him, he considered a patch of iris, nodded, and took one more leisurely step, his frayed rope dragging temptingly behind.

"Got him!" yelled Khalil inaccurately, diving for the rope. "*Bismallah!*" he added as it jerked searingly from his hands. By the time he had picked himself up again and retrieved his khaffiya and the double goat-hair cord that supposedly held it on his head, the goat was definitely disappearing over the crest of the hill, Yusif panting after it.

"Defilement of pigs!" muttered Khalil, gathering up the long folds of his *tob* and following. At times like this, he was inclined to think favorably of the Western trousers and shorts worn by the *Yahud*—the Jews—

and also by many town Arabs. Father disapproved, of
course, but then Father disapproved of anything new
or untraditional. There was no denying that long robes
could be inconvenient for things like chasing goats. He
turned to glance back at the rest of the herd, peacefully
grazing below, and hesitated. Dare he leave them? Suppose they decided to wander down into the valley? It
was an extremely broad, flat valley, stretching southward out of sight, ribboned with the Jordan river,
smudged with swamps, and dotted with both Arab and
Yahud villages. It gave tremendous scope to goats bent
on mischief . . .

"Khalil!" Yusif's urgent yell was accompanied by a
series of shouts, grunts, assorted scuffling noises, and
then a yelp. Forgetting his herd, Khalil launched himself over the brow of the hill almost as fast as the goat
had done.

Yusif and the black goat were engaged in brisk war-
fare with half a dozen Yahud soldiers, who seemed to
be getting the worst of it. Khalil, about to hurl himself
into the battle, paused for another look. There was no
doubt that Yusif and the goat had been the aggressors,
and still were. The black, bleating devil had butted
one man and was struggling with two more. Yusif's
idea, clearly, was to accomplish single-handedly what
the armies of six Arab nations had so far embarras-
singly failed to do in eighteen months of savage fighting all over Palestine—and that was to wipe the Yahud
off the face of the earth.

These particular Yahud, to Yusif's annoyance,

seemed not to appreciate the seriousness of their danger. Two had rifles, but held them very much at ease while they watched the antics of the goat. Another, grinning, held the small and infuriated warrior, who was flailing his arms and legs and repeating with remarkable accuracy the words Khalil had recently used. Then the grin was replaced by a look of pain, and the Yahudi shook a bitten hand. Khalil chuckled silently.

"Shalom!" called one of the other soldiers, seeing him. *"Salaam!"* he repeated in Arabic. "Peace!"

He seemed friendly in spite of being in the enemy army, but one never knew. The Yahud were tricky and treacherous. They didn't fight at all fairly, which was why they had not yet been conquered. Cunning must be matched by greater cunning, but at the moment Khalil was not sure what was needed. He stood still, noncommittal, ready to sell his life dearly if necessary.

Yusif was continuing his battle with unflagging energy. "Dogs of Yahud!" he panted, sure of immediate victory. "Pig-eaters!" he yelled untruthfully. "I shall slay thee all!"

The Yahud, not understanding Arabic, merely laughed and applauded him. Then, picking him up by the middle, they presented him courteously to Khalil. "Shalom," they repeated. "Salaam."

Khalil, cuffing Yusif to make him behave, regarded them with curiosity but very little warmth. Peace, indeed! Were the Yahud not trying to take Palestine for themselves? It was claimed that this was their homeland, long before the Arabs came, and also that it had been agreed in Father's youth when the Turks were driven forth and the English came, that Palestine should be a nation for the Jews. But it had been understood that these were mere words—until a year and a half ago (November of 1947 by the English calendar, said Iztar the cloth merchant), when some meddling country, or perhaps it was several countries, called UN had decided that the words should be made real. Palestine, they said, would not be entirely a Jewish state, but it would be divided into a Jewish and an Arab state.

This, of course, was quite insupportable. The Arabs in and around Palestine had very strong feelings about the matter, and very reasonably expressed them at once. So long as the English were still there, the strong feelings were expressed only in small ways, like ambushing the hated Yahud busses, or throwing bombs, or attacking their villages. A reasonable people would have got discouraged and gone away. But the Yahud showed no signs of being reasonable; on the contrary, they even started to shoot back. So when, in the spring just a year ago, the English all packed up and left, it was clearly necessary for the Arabs to take sterner measures, which they did by invading Palestine. From all around Palestine armies came, from Syria and Lebanon, Transjordan and Egypt, even Iraq and Saudi Arabia, to solve the problem of Palestine and the Yahud. For the solution, so said the Grand Mufti of

Jerusalem many times on the radio, was simple. Allah wished the Yahud exterminated to the last infant, and with His help it would take only two weeks, and then the Arabs would have all the land of Palestine for themselves.

What bitter arguments those broadcasts had stirred up! The small battered radio sat in the dimness of the village coffeehouse, where men spent much of the time sitting over cups of thick sweet coffee and listening, and arguing about what they heard. Yusif's grandfather, known to all the village as Kbeer Abou, had brooded over the radio with noisy excitement, even taking it home with him at night. Father merely sat stolidly smoking his water pipe, refusing to become concerned.

"*Mashallah!* Allah wills it!" Kbeer Abou echoed the radio. "We shall all go over this very hill to my fourth cousins in Syria, and there we shall stay while you join the army and help wipe out the cursed Yahud."

"Why?" grunted Father, at his most provoking.

"Why? Why? Because you are my son-in-law and I say so! And also because Haj Amin el Husseini, who is the Grand Mufti of Jerusalem and our spiritual leader, says so. You heard him. We will drive the descendants of pigs into the sea in a fortnight, and then all their lands and fields and settlements will be ours."

Father had sucked his pipe maddeningly. "You may be the father of my second wife," he conceded, "but it is I who am *mukhtar* of this village, and it is Mahmoud who is our *imam*. And neither Mahmoud nor Allah have told me to leave my village, nor even that Haj Amin el Husseini *is* our spiritual leader. On the other hand, Allah has given me a brain which tells me that the Husseini are an ambitious, corrupt, and murderous family who appoint themselves to high positions, and also that it is my duty to stay here and care for my village. Why did Allah place me here if He wished me elsewhere? And why did He permit the Yahud here if He wished them out?"

"He placed them here so that we could slay them!" Kbeer Abou fumed and argued. So, later, did the Syrian and Lebanese soldiers who came over the hills and spent whole evenings in the corner of the house where Father entertained guests. But Father's stubbornness was such as to make Mohammed's unmoving mountain seem a butterfly. Besides, by that time the Yahud had also taken to the radio, urging Palestine Arabs to stay neutral, and promising to let them alone. And since this was precisely what Father wanted, he chose to believe them. Presently he smashed the radio, saying that it was a wicked foreign machine which he never should have permitted in the village at all.

And so, although men from a few of the other villages along the hillsides had obediently abandoned their homes and joined the army, Bab-il-Howa had ignored the whole thing, and almost contrived to forget there was fighting going on at all. Achula Valley was a thumb jutting northward from the rest of Palestine,

wedged between Syria to the east and Lebanon to the
west. With hills on three sides, it didn't seem to be of
very great strategic importance, being almost a cul-de-
sac. True, the Yahud settlements scattered over the
valley floor had taken on a rather military character,
and tended to keep a watchful eye on the Arab villages
on the hills all around. And Arab armies had certainly
dominated the network of dusty roads some of the
time, at any rate. But the only violence to affect Bab-il-
Howa was incidental, when some Syrians became so
annoyed at Father that they staged a night raid and
killed all of Cousin Jawad's sheep. And since Jawad
hated the Yahud even more than did Kbeer Abou (if
this were possible), Father was able to point out reasonably that Allah had given a sign to indicate what
His will really was. This so infuriated Jawad that he
went off and joined the Syrian army, declaring that the
whole thing had been engineered by the Yahud,
helped a little by Shaitan.

But the "two weeks" the Grand Mufti talked about
had turned out to be very long ones indeed. After
many weeks instead, perhaps seventy, the Yahud were
still unexterminated, and the war dragged on. Or at
least Khalil supposed that it did, since these soldiers
were here and alive. But what were they doing up here
by the Lebanon border? Might they decide to kill a
couple of Arab boys who might reveal their presence?
Just a trifle uneasy, Khalil placed Yusif behind him
and looked defiant.

But the soldiers seemed far too amiable to be planning murder, unless they were more subtle than Khalil thought they were. Having wrestled the black goat to a standstill, they laughingly helped their fallen comrade to his feet. His laughter was wry, and he held his stomach, eyeing the goat. *"Ben Satan!"* he said in a heartfelt voice, in Hebrew.

The two languages being much alike, this needed no translation. Khalil's lip twitched. One couldn't help sympathizing a *little* with one of the black goat's victims, even an enemy one. *"Ibn Shaitan,* Son of Satan," he agreed, and then turned an interested eye upon the Yahud who had gone back to their interrupted task of unrolling barbed wire along the crest of the hill.

"What are you doing?" demanded Yusif, popping out from behind his half brother. "Who do you think you are, putting fences there? It is not your land; it belongs to Arabs, who will be very much annoyed when they come back, and will tear you limb from limb. Besides," he discovered, "that wire has got thorns in it, and it will be very inconvenient for anyone who wants to cross over the hill." And since these were very ignorant Yahud, who could not even understand simple Arabic, Yusif made his point quite clear by pointing to the barbed wire, scowling ferociously, and shaking his hard, round, black head.

Khalil regarded the barrier with sudden tolerance. It would also make things more difficult for the black goat. Still, it was puzzling to have Yahud putting it there. He paid interested attention to the short blond soldier who was trying to explain.

"Shalom," he was saying, which seemed rather silly under the circumstances. *"Eretz Israel. Chaverim. Is-raeli."* He waved his arms at his companions and then at the boys, who gazed at him with the kindly tolerance due to one whom Allah had made simple. He gazed back at them, frustrated. Then the man whom Yusif had bitten took over.

"Abba?" he asked, pointing to Khalil. *"Kfar?"*

Khalil at once recognized the Hebrew forms of the Arabic words *abou* and *kafer:* father and village. He turned and pointed to the spot along the northern range of hills where Bab-il-Howa lay, a sprawl of squat stone houses tucked into the flank of the hill as if growing there. Windows were few and tiny, giving the village a vague air of blindness. It stood out sharply in this brief green season, but for most of the year it was hard to see at a distance, tawny stone and dust and scorched grass all blending together, with only the silver-green of olive trees and a few bright fig trees showing clearly.

For some reason the Yahud seemed pleased that it was there. He nodded vigorously. *"Tov,"* he said. "Israeli." He waved an expansive hand at the valley. "Israel."

Khalil stared blankly at the scene below. To the east, the Jordan—little more than a stream among others—marked the beginning of foothills rising to the high

Syrian plateau. Westward the Lebanese border followed the Naphtali hills southward. It all looked the
same as ever, except for these soldiers and perhaps a
few other groups here and there. He shrugged, but
he couldn't help feeling sorry for these Yahud soldiers,
who were touchingly friendly, and who were doomed
to be massacred sooner or later. If only that UN hadn't
interfered, it would not be necessary, and things could
have gone on as they always had.

Suddenly remembering the rest of the herd, Khalil
hastily took a firm grip on the black goat's rope and his
neck hair as well, and headed back down the hill. Yusif
swaggered along, gripping a handful of black hair on
the other side, and describing his own heroism.

"—and did you see me fighting all those Yahud at
once, and barehanded?" he demanded. "I won, too,
and had them all crying for mercy before I stopped
biting and beating them. The goat helped a little," he
conceded generously, "but we had won before you
even got there." He stuck out his chest and strutted.

Khalil looked at him. Yusif sometimes bore a very
strong resemblance to his grandfather Kbeer Abou.

The sun was low when they finally started home-
ward along the slope of the hills. The western hills at
their backs were mauve, the eastern range amber in the
low light. Shadows began to fill the valley like water,
and a bird chittered softly. The afternoon breeze died,
and the air clung warm and still to sun-heated earth. It

was a fair land, surely loved by Allah, even though it was puzzling of Him to place too much water in the valley and not enough in the hills.

Yusif was still chattering, exalted by his adventure. "I don't think I shall go back to Mahmoud's school at all, for it is dull learning reading and the Koran, and now that I am a great warrior, I shall join the army instead. Won't Grandfather be pleased! Get along there, you devil goat, you! Why are you frowning, Khalil? Are you sorry we didn't kill all the Yahud? Never mind, we scared them very badly, and wounded some of them, and we can slay them later. Besides, I think those Yahud might not be so bad if they knew their place. They act," he pointed out with indignation, "as if they thought *they* were the Chosen of Allah and as good as Arabs! I think they should be taught a lesson about that."

Khalil was inclined to agree.

They came now to the olive grove, from which they could look down on the flat yellow-gray roofs of Bab-il-Howa, standing as they had stood for uncounted generations: so long that by now everyone was related to everyone else in a large clan with Father at the head.

Khalil looked down at it with an expression both affectionate and impatient. He wasn't sure why he was impatient, except that he longed for excitement and change. His best friend Selim wanted to go to a big city like Haifa and meet many people and learn everything in the world. Yusif wanted to conquer the world.

Khalil's ambitions were more modest and elastic. He merely wished to do something besides spend his life in this unchanging corner, tending goats and crops, eventually marrying and joining the men in the coffeehouse or playing chess under gaunt olive trees in a dusty courtyard; where the only excitement was that of a hot argument, a balking goat or mule, or a plague of sickness to carry off a fifth of the village . . .

As if to comment on his thoughts, an excited babble floated upward. Khalil listened, peered, placed a sandaled foot against the twisted gray trunk of an olive tree, and raised himself to where he could see the village street. It snaked downward in wide zigzags, neither paved nor cobbled, but with a mixture of dust and rock just as Allah had arranged them. The wide central gutter was dark with garbage, sewage, dead rats, and swarms of flies: a perfectly normal state of affairs, for where else would one put things not wanted indoors? Halfway down was the village center, where the road widened abruptly and opened to an almost-flat courtyard. Here was the market when there was one, here traveling merchants came, here was the dim little coffeehouse, and here villagers gathered.

They were gathered now, a disturbed hive, abuzz with fear and anger. Something had happened! "Come on!" said Khalil urgently, and began leading the goats down the narrow lane that branched in one direction to the fold and in the other between two houses to the village center. It was Yusif's job to prevent straggling and scattering at the rear—but Yusif had also heard the swarm below, and he had no sense of responsibility whatever.

"It's Iztar the cloth merchant with news!" he squealed, and instantly deserted his post, darting past Khalil's grasping hand and vanishing into the crowd at the bottom of the lane.

"Yusif!" bellowed Khalil uselessly, and grabbed the black goat just in time to prevent a stampede. Just wait until he caught that little bedbug! Fuming, he paused for just a frustrated instant at the fork of the lane. If only someone would see him and come bring the news, whatever it was! The buzzing had become a medley of shouts and wails such as he had not heard since the sweating sickness two years ago. But he dared neither desert his goats nor turn them loose in the village.

And then the crowd shifted and he was treated to the embarrassing sight of his twin sister Jasmin, veil half off the back of her head, burrowing into the crowd of men and boys as shamelessly as if she were a male or small child instead of a great grown girl of twelve. It was she who saw Khalil and responded to his need. Lifting her sand-colored *kaftan* far enough to show the bright trouser edges around slim ankles, she darted up the lane, alight with excitement.

"Oh, Khalil! What do you think has happened!"

Much as Kahlil wanted to know what had happened, this sort of behavior was too much to overlook. Jasmin had always been a thorn in his foot, anyway, and he was

not in a good mood at the moment. He regarded her
bleakly as she reached him, her small pointed face
vivid with news.

"*Ipe!*" he said sternly. "Shame! Look at you, standing around among men like a *Bedouine!* Go pray
Allah to forgive you!"

Animation instantly fled from Jasmin's face. People
were always saying ipe at her, especially since her last
birthday, and she found it very distressing. She had not
realized before that it was going to be quite so difficult
and so dull to become a woman. Everything the least
bit interesting was ipe, and she had for a long time
nursed a grievance toward Allah for creating such a
one-sided world. The grievance had begun almost in
babyhood, the first time a bewildered and indignant
little girl yelled vainly for equal advantages with her
twin brother. Now she knew her place in the scheme of
things—but she wasn't as fond of Allah as she ought
to be.

Arranging her face into the suitable mask of meekness and humility, Jasmin bent her head and studied
her twin through the conveniently thick veil of black
lashes. There was no doubt that he was passionately
curious. Good. She smiled behind her eyes.

"Forgive me, oh my brother," she murmured in con-
trite tones. "I obey at once." And she turned back
down the lane.

Khalil lowered suspicious brows. He never did trust
this sister of his, particularly when she was most hum-

ble. There was something decidedly odd about it;
something almost mocking, although he could never
quite put his finger on it, and it was quite unthinkable
for a female to mock a male. Or at least it ought to be
unthinkable. Khalil kept finding himself thinking it.
Perhaps it was the dark gleam from beneath those
heavy lids—or the fact that however submissively her
black head was bent, that slender back always remained defiantly straight. Bismallah, but there was a
demon within her! Always, all their lives, she had
somehow challenged his superiority.

He scowled, remembering that he still had to take
the goats to the fold, and he wanted to hear the news,
and Jasmin was definitely walking away. Not rapidly—
but definitely.

"Stay!" he commanded. Jasmin stopped where she
was, her back still turned. "As long as you have come,"
he went on, elaborately casual, "you may as well tell
me what has happened."

Jasmin didn't turn. "It is nothing, oh my brother."

"Tell me anyway!" Khalil began to simmer. She had
somehow got him where she wanted him again. It was
unnatural. Males should always keep the upper hand
over females. The difficulty was in keeping what one
had never really got. "Speak!"

Slim shoulders shrugged. "Oh, nothing, really. Only
that Iztar brings news that the war is ended."

Khalil snorted. "Then he is mistaken," he scoffed.
"For Yusif and I have just seen Yahud soldiers on the

hill, very much alive, and not even driven into the sea."

"But I did not say that they had been killed or driven out," returned his sister, turning a dark head to look at him. Her eyes were glowing with something not in the least respectful or meek. "Iztar has not said we won the war, oh my brother. He said the Yahud won. And that means that we are now living in the Yahud nation of Israel."

2. JASMIN

Jasmin marched triumphantly back down the lane, so elated at scoring on Khalil that she almost forgot the disastrous news. As a matter of fact, the news had not yet touched her with any sense of reality—but her contest with Khalil was in an odd way the most real thing in her life. It was her fight for identity: for the right to be a separate person instead of just a female and the daughter, sister, mother of males. Not that Jasmin in the least knew why she was so driven. She only knew that the contest had gone on, unacknowledged, since the day Khalil started to Mahmoud's little school and she was expected, instead, to learn to balance a piece of sacking on her head.

Since a brief and bitter rebellion had earned nothing but punishment, Jasmin had gone underground. She now waged her war behind the role of submissive female, from where she kept Khalil in a state of great annoyance.

At the bottom of the lane she glanced over her shoulder to see him staring after her with a familiar expression of incredulous suspicion. Then the black goat made a determined effort to join the crowd, Khalil grabbed him, and Jasmin was forced to flatten herself back against the wall as a surge of people rushed up the hill to tell their mukhtar and imam, bearing Iztar the cloth merchant in their midst.

Jasmin joined the fringes and followed, listening to the cries and shouts and wails, beginning to be infected with the panic herself.

"Allah save us! . . . They will slay us all! . . . Nay, the news must be false, for Allah would never permit Unbelievers to triumph . . . Perhaps it is a wicked Yahud lie spread to alarm us . . . It must be a clever trick of our leaders, who will sign this armistice thing and then attack and wipe out the Yahud when they are not expecting it . . . But if we are now in Yahud land, they will come wipe us out first!"

They had now reached the high stone wall before the mukhtar's house, at the top of the village, and were beginning to call for him. Jasmin reluctantly began to sidle through the crowd—very slowly, so as to hear as much as possible. Listening to talk was the only way she could ever learn anything, and she made the most of it, thankful to be the mukhtar's daughter and in the center of important things. And certainly this was the most important thing that had *ever* happened! She swallowed hard, reached the gate, and paused, for Iztar was speaking, filled with morbid self-importance.

"It is said that perhaps the Yahud will not slay *all* of

us, but only drive us forth from our lands and villages, and over the borders to be beggars in neighbor lands."

A renewed wail went up, and the back of the crowd pressed the front right through the mukhtar's gate. "Moussa, Moussa!" rose the cry. "Mahmoud!" And they swept into the small courtyard with its grape-covered trellis and gnarled olive tree, a small table under it with the chess game waiting for Father and Mahmoud, half a dozen hysterical chickens, and a motherless kid tethered to the tree.

Father was doubtless out in the back part of the house tending the sore paw of Buazza the dog. Jasmin had been now pushed right to the front door, and there was no longer an excuse for lingering, but she paused all the same, leaning against the faded blue paint of the wood—(blue to keep out evil spirits) her eyes now wide with apprehension.

"The villagers of Daya Bir," added Iztar, "are even now abandoning their homes and crossing into Lebanon."

That brought the fear close and real indeed. Jasmin caught her breath. A groan arose from the crowd, echoed just inside the crack of the blue door. Jasmin slipped inside, and was not greatly surprised to find Zubaida, her mother, and Hayat, Father's young third wife, just on the other side, listening anxiously. Silently they moved to make room for her.

"By the beard of the Prophet!" cried the voice of Uncle Rashid, a plaintive man ruled firmly by his second wife Basna, although he had not yet noticed this. "I think that no one cares what happens to us! Our leaders have betrayed us! They promised us quick victory and all the Yahud property, and instead they give us defeat and the loss of our own, and then they run away to safety and leave us at the mercy of the enemy! A curse on them all!"

Defeat! It was a galling word, rising edgily through the general fear, searing Arab pride.

"It isn't true!" cried Hassoun, a very striking young man with a sharply sloping forehead, a jutting chin, and an exceedingly high opinion of himself. He had been saying all along how much he wanted to go fight the Yahud. Jasmin had noticed, however, that he only talked about it and never did it.

"It is true!" asserted Iztar with dogged indignation. "Our armies have all left, as I told thee, every man of them; and Egypt and Jordan and Lebanon have all now signed the armistice papers, and Syria will do so presently, as soon as it is agreed. And this valley, which was before part of Palestine, will now be part of the Yahud nation."

It sounded terribly convincing, and most ominous. Jasmin's stomach felt odd, and Hayat whimpered a little, and even calm Mother stirred nervously. Outside, voices rose again, frightened and angry. "We had better leave at once! . . . We can cross into Lebanon . . . Here is the mukhtar; what shall we do, oh, Moussa?"

And then Father's deep voice, banishing panic. "Listen to me, my friends. Perhaps this news is true and perhaps not. Whichever it is must be the will of Allah, is it not so, Mahmoud?"

"*Il mektub mektub:* what is written is written," replied the high sweet voice of the imam. "One cannot run from Destiny."

Moussa followed the words closely with his own. "And think ye that Allah's will cannot cross the border? Nay, friends, we shall remain here and await events. Perhaps the news is false, or even if it is true, the Yahud promised not to harm those who have remained at peace with them, and they show no sign of breaking this promise. I remember, it mattered very little when I was young and the Turks went away and the English ruled over us instead. Perhaps it will not matter now."

"Matter!" Kbeer Abou had hurried up the street on wizened legs, his tob flapping about bony ankles, *aba* streaming behind, khaffiya askew, to have his say. "Matter! Shall we be conquered by foreigners, by accursed Yahud? Never! It is a trick of Shaitan, a false story spread by demons, and besides, it is impossible. We have always been conquerors, ruling all other people!" he bawled, his wispy gray beard wagging with emotion. Kbeer Abou was unhampered by any notions of logic, fact, or likelihood. He believed in anything that sounded well at the time, could entertain as many as a dozen impossible ideas at once, and frequently did so.

"Are we not the Sons of the Prophet? Are we not the strongest, fiercest, most glorious people on earth? Can anyone deny it? Are we sheep? Are we to call the accursed Jews master? Allah forbid! Where is the glory of Islam?"

Through the shouts of the easily-swayed villagers, Jasmin could almost see Father shrug his massive shoulders. "Allah, it seems, did not forbid," he pointed out drily. "Why argue until we know more? Ye who are very greatly frightened can no doubt follow our landlord into Syria. He is rich. Perhaps he needs more servants there. As for me, I shall remain here and attend to my business."

It was his final word: that was perfectly clear. And he might come inside at any moment. His wives and daughter hurried from behind the door and set about neglected tasks.

The mukhtar's house was, quite rightly, the finest in the village. The donkey and oxen and chickens lived quite separately in the back (even though this made it less warm in winter), and the whole large room was for the family. At one end there was a little curtained alcove for female privacy, and at the other, on a raised bit of floor, Father's special corner where he entertained guests, or sat and smoked his water pipe, or talked with Mahmoud. His bed-mat folded back to make a fine sitting mat, and there were cushions and a low table.

Along the back wall there stood the rows of jars and

pots and storage bins of olives, beans, raisins, flour, grain, oil, rice, dried chick-peas, and coffee beans, ranged on either side of the hearth. There were piles of wooden plates and bowls, the stone mill for grinding the grain into flour, a copper pan for roasting coffee beans, tiny cups.

Two small windows were cut high in the stone walls, which were some three feet thick and covered with mud plaster. The roof was dome-shaped inside, but it had been made flat on top, and stairs went up the outside wall, and in the long hot season they all ate and sat and even slept up there.

Jasmin's mother had hurried to begin the evening meal, while Hayat picked up her fretting baby. The little thing did not take at all kindly to swaddling, and she had Jasmin's complete sympathy. Even the submissive Hayat looked unhappy about it.

"I wish—" she began, and then stopped, very much aware of her position as a very young and foolish wife. Moussa had married her only a year ago, after Yusif's mother and three of his children died in the sweating sickness, and she still felt very much overwhelmed.

Jasmin, often scornful of Hayat's excessive tameness, this time gave her a sympathetic grin, poked her half sister gently in her fat tummy, and went to help Mother.

"Thou wert a long time out," observed Zubaida without surprise, beginning to mash the soaked chick-peas for *humus*. "Olive oil."

Jasmin handed it to her and began to cut slices of white, dry goat's cheese and fill bowls with yoghurt. "I stopped to hear the news," she explained just a shade defiantly. "And then I saw Khalil, and told him about it."

Zubaida regarded her daughter with a familiar mixture of compassion and apprehension. Why, she often wondered, had Allah seen fit to place the spirit of a boy in the body of a girl? She was afraid for Jasmin, for the banked fires behind her eyes might at any time blaze up out of control. "I hope Kbeer Abou did not see thee," was all she said, pouring out rice for the *mausaf*.

"Bismallah! So do I!" Jasmin agreed earnestly. "Khalil scolded me once, and that's enough for one evening." Her lips curled upward in glee as she remembered the satisfying encounter. Almost at once they curled down again. "Mother, what do you think will happen? If the—"

"Shhh!" said Zubaida as Moussa entered, followed by the still yammering Kbeer Abou. Between them they made an atmosphere very much like thunder and lightning, as they seated themselves on their mats. Jasmin took one look at her father and felt more frightened than ever. His black-bearded face was as impassive as always—but Jasmin knew the qualities of his impassiveness. He believed the news; she could tell. He was upset and angry and worried. So, instantly, was she. She watched him from under her lashes while her hands went on preparing the supper.

He had wrapped himself in dark thought, paying no more attention to his father-in-law than to the hundreds of flies buzzing in lazy circles about the room, both being annoyances that it had somehow pleased Allah to create and tolerate.

Kbeer Abou, thin beard and thick eyebrows jutted forth, was in one of his most fire-eating moods. He was a great warrior, was Kbeer Abou—in speech. He had a great deal to say about slaying Infidels in general and Yahud in particular for the greater glory of Allah, and he always had excellent reasons why someone else should do the dangerous part. Presently he shouted himself into merciful silence and sat simmering darkly. Jasmin shot him a poisonous look. She disliked him very much indeed. In addition to all his other unlovable qualities, he kept saying that twins were bad luck, females a curse, and that Jasmin should certinly have been buried alive at birth according to old Koranic custom. She wished a scorpion or viper would bite him.

Brown silence hovered while her oldest brother Ahmed came in, bringing a kind of peace with him. Quite probably he had never yet given a thought to anything but his family and the crops, and never would. He was stolid and patient and silent and kind, and Jasmin loved him very much.

Next came Khalil, blazing with a rage that Jasmin didn't understand. Being a girl, she didn't share the unbearable humiliation of Arab males in knowing themselves defeated . . . and not merely defeated, but thoroughly, shamefully whipped by a mere handful of ill-armed men—*and women!*—against six well-equipped armies including the highly trained troops of the Arab Legion that the English had left behind. It simply wasn't endurable, or even believable! But after one look at his elders, Khalil prudently decided that this was not the moment to express his feelings. Instead, he looked threateningly at Yusif, who, being quite insensitive to such things, didn't notice, but bounced cheekily up to his grandfather, who cuffed him. Yusif, used to spoiling from that direction, stuck out an aggrieved lip and passed the blow on to Jasmin, who clenched her fists and promised herself vengeance at a later and safer moment.

Yusif was a great trial to Jasmin. He possessed no manners, no conscience, and a perfectly shattering sense of his own superiority. And although a good hard smack sometimes won his respect for a moment or two, nothing would ever shake his conceit. Just now he was feeling outraged at being still classed with women and children, who waited while men ate first. He, a great warrior, who had only this day slain three or perhaps twelve Yahud soldiers with his bare hands! Moreover, he now knew a number of splendid manly words.

"Kus emmek," he murmured experimentally. "Kus emmek," he repeated with relish. "Kus emmek, kus emmek!"

His father looked at him suddenly, eyes glittering dangerously under the hedge of his brows. Yusif hastily scuttled to safety behind the protective robes of Zubaida. Perhaps it was as well to wait, after all, before joining the men at their meals. They were in an unreasonable humor today.

Jasmin placed a steaming bowl of mausaf on the low table between the squatting men and withdrew silently. She was feeling more and more alarmed. Perhaps the Yahud really might come and massacre them all? She didn't at all like the quality of Father's silence. It was a relief when he broke it, eyes fixed gravely upon Kbeer Abou.

"*Ya Abou,*" he began, "Thou art the father of my second wife, and it is right that I respect thee."

"By Allah, that is true!" agreed the old man with energy, and the gray beard tilted challengingly.

"Nevertheless," Moussa went on, "I and not you am Mukhtar of this village, and for the sake of the village I have a thing to say. This is a difficult time and tempers are raw. I think if violence comes to Bab-il-Howa, it will be thy hot talk that sets it off."

Kbeer Abou looked pleased. "By the beard of the Prophet, I think you are right! We will begin with violence here, and then spread it to all the villages, and presently there will be war again, and this time we shall win. Our armies lacked inspiration and leadership before," he discovered. "This time I shall furnish inspiration, and thou will at last heed my wisdom and do as I say." He plunged his hand into the bowl of mausaf and withdrew it filled with the rice and meat mixture. Not a drop spilled on his beard, although he nodded happily as he ate.

Moussa frowned. "I want no violence in my village!" he thundered. "We have gone through the war without it, minding our own business, and we shall continue to do so!"

"Sheep!" squealed the old man, in a sudden fury. "If only I were young and strong, I would show thee what it is to fight! Only," he added hastily, "I am much too old now. The younger generation are all sheep and mice and jackals." He took an enormous bite of *pita* and lapsed into sullen gobbling, from which he emerged presently to storm out of the house, mouth full. Presently he would be preaching a Holy War at the coffeehouse, and to a largely sympathetic audience.

Moussa finished eating. The women and children gathered around the small table and had their own meal, depressed and silent. Jasmin began to be devoured with a passion of curiosity. What was it all about, anyway? Who had a right to what, and why? If only someone would explain! . . . She looked speculatively at her father, who had finished his coffee and was now meditating over the bubbling of his water-pipe. Sometimes if approached in just the right way . . .

Yusif, unafflicted by the atmosphere of impending disaster, scampered out to tell his friends about the fifty Yahud soldiers he had slain. Khalil, smouldering, went out to find comfort or feed his anger, depending on whether he talked to Selim or Hassoun. The women cleared up, glancing at their lord and master and raising hopeful and inquiring eyebrows at one another. Mostly Zubaida and Hayat looked at Jasmin. Moussa had a very soft spot for his elder daughter, and if anyone could stick her head into the lion's mouth with impunity, guess who it was?

Jasmin made a great show of martyrdom, which impressed no one. She enjoyed the challenge and they knew it. So presently she went and knelt beside the massive figure, a very picture of daughterly respect and affection.

"My father?" she ventured.

His eyes came back from far distances and rested on her, brooding, troubled, angry. Then they softened. Encouraged, Jasmin went on in a tumble of words.

"Father, *are* the Yahud going to come kill us or drive us forth?"

Tense silence, and then he smiled comfortingly, and stroked her shining black hair. "No," he said firmly. "They are not a warlike or vengeful people. Moreover, they have kept peace with us during the war; why should they break faith now?"

It was what he had already told the villagers, but now that he told *her,* Jasmin's fear dropped away in one simple swoop. Her faith in her father was profound and unquestioned. She gave an enormous sigh and smiled at him trustfully. He smiled back, touched, and she quickly seized the moment of his mellowness.

"I don't understand, Father," she complained. "Why did we fight at all? Whose land *is* it? If it's Arab land, how is it that the English ruled it, and the Turks before them; and how can people like our landlord own bits of it and sell it to Yahud if someone else owns all of it? And did the English and Turks buy it, too? And if they didn't, why did they rule it? And what business is it of this UN, anyway?"

Moussa took the stem of his pipe from his mouth and stared right through her for a moment, at the row of storage jars opposite. He had forgotten that she was only a girl—which was precisely what Jasmin had hoped he would do. He responded merely to an inquiring mind, asking some of the same questions he asked himself, deserving an intelligent attempt at an answer.

"A nation is land," he rumbled at last, pursuing the thread of his own reflections. "Land is earth, to plow and to live on, as our fathers have done before us, according to Allah's will. What, then, does it matter who claims to rule it, or even own it? Men fight and argue and sign papers and draw borders like that on top of the hills, but the land is the same on both sides of the hill, and life goes on, and all I ask is to be left alone to live it. As to the Yahud, it is true that they are Unbelievers, but they are not so bad. They have been coming here for a very long time, buying bad land for much money, but making it into good land, and for that I respect them even though they pay too much and let themselves be cheated. As for the UN, I know nothing about them or where they live or by what right they divided Palestine between Yahud and Arab. If they leave us alone, what does it matter?"

Jasmin thought about it. "Well, it might matter to

our landlord," she suggested shrewdly. "Will he come back, even though this is now Yahud land? And how will he collect his share of the crops if he stays in Syria?"

Moussa forgot to put his pipe back in his mouth. He stared at her, having suddenly remembered who she was. The dark eyes were huge with interest. Surely so much thinking was unnatural and could not be good for her? Bismallah! It would give her the headache for days!

"Don't trouble thy head about such things, child," he soothed. "There's no need. Thy life is to be a good daughter and then a good wife, and to find happiness bearing man-children to thy husband."

Jasmin found the prospect less than satisfying. Her chin shot forward in a way that forcefully reminded the watching Zubaida of Moussa. Then she remembered hard-learned lessons in strategy, and drooped her head in mock submissiveness. "Yes, my father," she murmured. "But, Father, I can't help wondering a *little* about such things, so isn't it better if you explain to me what I should think? Otherwise I might accidentally believe Kbeer Abou or someone."

He looked at her sharply. But those wide eyes were surely free of guile? It was innocence speaking aloud, and he beetled his eyebrows, since it would not at all do to laugh at her. "I have told thee quite enough for now," he said. "Surely there are tasks for thee to do?" And he pulled his beard thoughtfully as she sighed, arose, and glided away. A good daughter, obedient and intelligent as well as pretty. A pity she was a— But one must not question the ways of Allah. She would make a fine wife and mother, and would soon outgrow a tendency to rather more spirit and curiosity than was really becoming to a female. She was the least of his worries.

Having reassured his village and his daughter, Moussa himself lay awake that night, deeply uneasy. All very well to point out that the Yahud were peace-loving. So were most people in times of peace. But whatever he might say to others, in his mind he did not evade the fact that the Arabs had attacked the Jews for the avowed purpose of total extermination. And unspeakable things had happened to Yahud, living or dead, who fell into Arab hands. It would not be really astonishing if—

Moussa felt a slow, burning anger toward the Arab leaders who had started all of this and now left others to bear any possible consequences. He had never trusted their promises. He very much hoped Allah would see fit to punish them appropriately, and to protect His innocent people.

But it never once occurred to Moussa to leave his village. His roots were generations deep; they would never grow elsewhere.

3. no machines

Bab-il-Howa seethed and simmered. Women clustered on doorsteps and at the spring up on the hillside; men grouped in the coffeehouse and courtyard. Even children caught the waves of fear, shame, anger, disbelief that swept conflictingly over the village. Khalil brooded blackly all the way to pasture, not sure whether he was most infuriated at the Yahud, the Arab armies, or perhaps Fate itself.

Selim, now recovered from his sickness, watched with understanding eyes in his olive face and said nothing. The trouble with Khalil, he decided astutely, was too much conceit and not enough. He needed to feel superior, but—unlike Yusif and Kbeer Abou—lacked the colossal vanity to be sure of it. And he was too intelligent to be able to believe a thing just because he wanted to. So he was always at war within himself, and resentful of anything that might challenge his self-esteem.

It was why he couldn't get along with Jasmin, whom Selim liked very much. Selim wondered if Khalil would ever be able to forgive the Yahud for defeating them.

"Wallah!" exploded Khalil presently, staring with hot eyes down the valley where Yahud activity was again evident. "Shaitan must have helped them!"

Selim looked judicious. "Even with Shaitan, they couldn't have done it if Allah hadn't approved," he pointed out. "Perhaps He wishes us to live in Yahud country for some reason, or even to try some of the new Yahud ways . . . like trousers or machinery . . ."

And then he fell silent again, leaving the magic word to do its work. Khalil was passionately interested in machines . . .

The boys would have been very much upset had they known that, down on the valley floor, their sisters were even now having an adventure.

The two girls had gone out for fuel, wandering much further than either of their mothers would have approved, Jasmin balancing her large basket easily on her head while small Katan, just learning, pattered anxiously beside her. Katan had worn the sacks on her head for some time now, but this was the first time she had tried a real basket with something useful in it. A ring of sacking rested around the crown of her head to help balance, and she gazed admiringly at Jasmin, who was a big girl and no longer needed it.

"I shall soon be able to carry water jars, shan't I?" she asked hopefully, almost tipping her basket off as she peered into Jasmin's face. "Yusif can't do this, can he?" she added with a kind of forlorn defiance that Jasmin at once recognized. "And he can't really read at all well, no matter how he brags," she finished, truculent.

Jasmin stooped swiftly, basket of dung still securely balanced. "Katan!" She searched the small flower face, oval and almond-eyed like Selim's. "Do you want to learn to read, too?"

Katan looked alarmed for an instant, but Jasmin's face reassured her, and she nodded so violently that her basket at once fell off. Both girls ignored it. For all the five years difference between them, they had just discovered kindred spirits, trapped and lonely in girls' bodies.

"Probably you have devils in you, too," Jasmin decided sadly. "You'd better not tell anybody, Katan. I know. I tried to learn when Khalil did, and I even got him to teach me a few letters, just at first, when he was showing off. But then when he found I was learning them, he wouldn't show me any more, and I got another scolding. You'd be better if you could just forget the whole thing, Katan."

Katan's eyes were wide at being talked to like a grown-up human being—and by the wholly wonderful Jasmin, too! But she shook her head.

"How can you forget if it keeps pushing in your head?" she asked reasonably, and bent to pick up her scattered cakes of dried dung and sticks. There was no answer to this. Jasmin helped refill the basket, placed it firmly on the curly dark head, and they set off again along the dusty track of a road, back toward Bab-il-Howa.

The sound of an engine made them both turn. It was not a very common sound this far up the valley. Yahud settlements were not very close, and Father had made it clear even before the war that while he believed in live and let live, he also preferred neighbors with newfangled ideas to be out of sight and out of mind.

"Patrol?" guessed Jasmin.

But the jeep that came around the bend didn't look like a patrol. One of the men looked like that Captain Granott who had come last year to talk with Father about staying neutral. He was a nice man, and a friend, for he had been given coffee, and there was no doubt in Jasmin's mind that he knew the answers to some of the things that puzzled her about the Yahud.

Jasmin wasn't so bold as to hold out her hand for the jeep to stop, but she might just as well have done so. No signal could have been more definite than the two faces—one oval and one pointed—shining like candles with curiosity.

The young Jewish driver had slowed down, and now raised questioning blue eyes to his superior officer. Having been born and raised in Palestine, he knew how very touchy Arabs were about their women and girls. One might easily offend an entire village. And yet—

"Stop a respectful distance away," ordered the captain, leaning forward to stare. "Not sure, but I think that's Moussa's daughter. Noticed her particularly when I visited before. The child blazes with energy; ought to be a Jew."

The jeep halted diffidently, so that the graying head was clearly visible in the passenger seat and a flaming red one behind the wheel. Two pairs of dark eyes rounded even further, and when it was seen that the eyes below that unlikely hair were of an intense blue, Katan could contain herself no longer.

"Wallah!" she cried, clutching at Jasmin's hand in alarm. "The Evil Eye!"

Jasmin wavered, but stood her ground. It *was* the nice captain, and he had paid the astonishing tribute of stopping to greet them, and there was no one else from the village in sight. Surely not even Aunt Sarika would be so poor-spirited as to run away now! Or at least she undoubtedly would, but Jasmin wouldn't. Greatly daring, she stood still and surveyed the men with tremendous and grave interest.

"Salaam," said the captain politely. "Are you not the mukhtar's daughter?"

Jasmin nodded. Katan recovered from her fright and pointed a small brown hand. "Has he got the Evil Eye?" she demanded, nothing if not direct.

"Not a bit," said the officer. "I wouldn't have him for my driver if he did. You see, this particular shade of blue is quite the opposite from evil. It's called the Glad Eye, and it is said to be very good luck indeed to know someone who has it."

Jasmin nodded again, perfectly satisfied, and went on to the next question. "If it is true that you have won the war, then who owns our village now; the Yahud or our landlord?" she asked. "And why did the English go away?"

Both men looked startled. Such forthrightness from an Arab girl was astonishing. Jasmin's face flamed suddenly as the impropriety of her conduct swept over her. Her hand gripped Katan's, but her bare brown feet stayed firmly planted where they were.

"Those are very complicated questions, Daughter of Moussa," said the captain apologetically. "It would take a long time to answer them properly, but I can tell thee that we will try our very best to be fair to all, even your landlord who abandoned his property in order to take up arms against us."

Jasmin considered this. "I don't think he ought to have his property back," she said judiciously. "I hope you don't let him come back, for he is greedy and unfair, and no one likes him." Then she ducked her head and peered out with sudden shyness through the veil of her lashes. It was typical of her that she forgot all about her proper veil of white cloth, which instead of modestly covering her lower face in the presence of strange men was hanging as usual half off the back of her head. "Please," she added earnestly, "could you— That is, will you—"

She couldn't quite say it. But Katan could. "Please will you not tell anybody we spoke to you?" she asked trustfully.

Gray eyes twinkled in his square, tanned face. "Certainly I won't. It is no part of my official business, and besides, I have already forgotten. I very much wish we could offer to drive you back to your village, but—" He cocked his head and raised an eyebrow.

"Bismallah!" bleated the girls, visualizing the effect of such a return. But Jasmin giggled, and Katan was half ready to face the consequences in order to lord it over Yusif just once. Two pairs of wistful eyes followed the jeep's progress up the hill.

"Oh, Jasmin," sighed Katan. "Don't you *wish* we *could?*"

"Yes," said Jasmin with pure and hopeless desire.

Hurry as they might, the girls missed the dramatic arrival of the jeep in the village, surrounded by scared but dazzled children, squealing excitedly about massacres and Evil Eyes. Mothers lurked in doorways fingering amulets and calling their children in tones of alarm, but mostly for form's sake. On the whole there was more resentment than fright—especially since there were only two Yahud, who did not look very dangerous.

The jeep halted in front of the coffeehouse, unable to go further had it wished, and Moussa came out. His bearded face was a mask, his greeting was formal and sonorous. By the time Jasmin and Katan came panting up the hill, the two men were walking up toward the mukhtar's house leaving the fascinating jeep and red-haired driver to be the object of spellbound interest. Kbeer Abou cowered behind the coffeehouse door, clutching his amulet and chittering about Evil Eyes. Hassoun and his Yahud-hating friends were invisible. None of them were likely to do or say anything rash, being very discreet warriors indeed, who would never commit the imprudence of attacking anything remotely capable of fighting back.

Jasmin never needed to be reminded of her duties when Father had guests. Abandoning her basket of fuel, she picked up her robes and raced by back lanes; and when Moussa and the captain arrived there was a perfect scene of domestic propriety. Two wives, veiled and silent, had coffee beans ready to roast in the brass skillet while a rather breathless daughter demurely tended the baby in the far corner. There was not, of course, the faintest glimmer of suggestion that she and the guest had ever seen each other—or did so now. It would have been atrocious manners for a guest to look at his host's women at all, and they moved and worked in an aura of invisibility.

The two men sat cross-legged on cushions, each with a bolster at his elbow, while the roasted beans were being pulverized in the wooden mortar. Conversation was polite nothing until three cups had been consumed with courteous slurps of enjoyment from the Yahud. Jasmin wriggled impatiently, aboil with interest.

"I have a difficult task, oh Moussa ibn Farid," said

Captain Granott at last, with a sudden smile at his host. "I must speak two kinds of words to thee." He paused and Moussa nodded. "First, the State of Israel welcomes its Arab citizens. We will give peace and equality and justice to all alike, as we have promised."

There was something about face or voice that caused Moussa's eyes to narrow shrewdly. "But—" he prompted.

"But," agreed the captain with a wry smile. "I think it is not an unreasonable but, oh Mukhtar. It is that we also expect you to keep the peace and abide by our laws."

Moussa looked affronted, quite deliberately. It was good Arab policy to keep the offensive. Anyone who gave ground could expect to be pushed still further back. That was the rule of life. "What laws?" he demanded truculently. "We need no foreign laws. We have our own customs which we do not seek to impose on you, and we desire that you let us live without interference."

Captain Granott sighed. "There will be no unnecessary interference, but there must be laws. Every nation must have order. Time does not flow backwards, oh Mukhtar, and tomorrow cannot always be the same as yesterday. Israel will have new laws even as Palestine had them when the English took rulership from the Turks. But there will be benefits as well."

Moussa jutted his lips out. "And if we wish neither laws nor benefits?"

"One of the benefits will be your right to vote and elect men to *Knesset* to try to change laws you do not like."

Frowning, Moussa put his finger squarely on the weakness. "You will make me adopt new ways in order to avoid new ways," he complained. "Moreover, you have not mentioned what these laws and benefits will be."

Jasmin in her corner leaned forward, pleased with the prospect of anything new and interesting. Captain Granott smiled again at her father. "Well, I can't yet tell you exactly. We're only starting to get organized, you know. But there will be the usual laws about crimes, about government, about education and marriage and sanitation. As soon as possible we hope to have medical treatment and schools available for all, and one of the first things will be to bring pure water in pipes to every home, and drains and cesspools for sewage."

In the back corner, the females exchanged puzzled glances, not altogether pleased. If water came into houses, how could they meet and talk to their friends every day at the spring? Moussa didn't look overjoyed, either.

"Why?" he demanded. "We have a spring on the hillside, a river in the valley, cisterns in the village and drains in our street." What more did anyone need? "Why should we have water in pipes?"

"Because other water is sometimes dirty and evil,"

the captain explained. "It can make people sicken and die."

This was greeted by four incredulous frowns. Everyone knew that devils caused sickness, and that everything that happened was by the will of Allah. (Jasmin privately felt a little muddled about these two things, but that was because she was only a girl and not very clever.) How, then, could water cause sickness? The whole idea was not merely foolish, but also, said Moussa, it indicated highhanded interference of the grossest nature. "Why cannot you ignore us as the Turks did?"

"They took very heavy taxes from you, did they not?"

This was true. Moussa meditated it. "And what of you? Will you not also take taxes? Or do you take the land itself?" He remembered Jasmin's question. "What of our landlord, who has fled into Syria? Shall we still pay him rent, or do the Yahud steal his land?"

Did the captain just barely flicker an eyelid in Jasmin's direction? She rather thought so. "It is a difficult situation," he admitted. "We have not yet worked it out. His land is his, but it is also in Israel, and he cannot very well pack it up and take it to Syria with him, spring and orchard and village and all."

There was a muffled giggle from the corner. Moussa chose not to hear it. He permitted his lips to curl slightly in acknowledgment of the joke. "And?"

"We can only pay such people for their land, as soon

as the present armistices become truces and we can sit down with our neighbors and arrange such matters as fairly as possible."

This struck Moussa as being extraordinarily generous. What nation beats off aggressor armies and then recompenses the enemy for its losses? Ridiculous! Was it some kind of clever trick, or had Allah softened the wits of the Yahud? Or—most likely—were they trying to placate the Arabs? If so, Moussa didn't find it at all admirable. One admired strength, Conquerors should behave as such, not as fawning dogs. His face hardened, looked almost contemptuous.

"In the meantime," said Captain Granott in a brisk military voice that made Jasmin jump, "I must warn you that border areas such as this must remain under military law until we are sure they are secure. It is forbidden to cross the border in either direction, or to communicate across it, or to assist anyone else to do these things. I know this is hard on those with relatives on the other side—but it is necessary. And if you should want to travel outside the area of your village, it will be necessary for you to come to us and get a piece of paper called a permit." He looked quite calmly at his host's scowl and smiled a little. "You are not a stupid man, Moussa ibn Farid; you know quite as well as I that these things are necessary and why. Already there have been raids across the borders, and some of our people slain."

It was the kind of speaking, now, that Moussa could

respect, however little he might like it. His back straightened, dignity gathered around him like an aura, but he could not honestly be offended. Instead he inclined his head like royalty making a concession. "Then it is not true that you intend to drive us from our villages?" The question was casual, as befitted such a momentous one.

"I certainly hope not!" His guest leaned forward, intensely earnest. "Not unless a village makes trouble, conspires with enemies across the border, and forces us to move them inland. Guard thine own people, Mukhtar, for the sake of all of us!" He started to rise and take his leave. Then another thought struck him. "Oh, by the way, there will be new neighbors for thee soon. Some of our young people come to build a new village along the hill not far away."

"To keep an eye on—things?" suggested Moussa drily.

"As you say," his guest agreed, equally dry. Both pairs of eyes twinkled a trifle. They began quite to like each other. Then Captain Granott made a tactical error. "They will have all sorts of modern machines and methods to improve crops, by the way, and will be happy to help you—"

Moussa bristled, both pride and conservatism outraged. "I do not want Yahud help, or ideas, or machines! Machines are ugly, and stink, and make evil noises to pollute the air; they are an offense to mankind and against the will of Allah."

Jasmin, quivering with excitement, had to be hauled back to her sitting position by her mother's hand on the back of her kaftan. What drama! What a scene! What would happen next?

"Are your wooden plows against the will of Allah?" asked Captain Granott, mildly surprised. "Our machines are only larger and better plows."

Moussa merely shook his head scornfully. There was a brief and frustrated silence.

"On the way up the hill," remarked the guest thoughtfully, "I saw a woman of your village in front of her house. She was cooking in a gasoline tin over a small dung fire. I think it was sorrel soup, which is not very nourishing.

"The children around her were very thin," he continued, "and I think that some of them will surely die before they grow up, either from hunger or from disease that they are not strong enough to resist. Is this, too, the will of Allah?"

"Of course," said Moussa, surprised but also slightly uncomfortable.

"And if I were to offer those children food, would you then strike it from their lips?"

"Nay, for then it would be the will of Allah that you feed them." Moussa's eyes glimmered, enjoying his own retort. But only for an instant.

"But then how do you know tractors are not also the will of Allah?"

Dark eyes and light ones clashed. Light ones smiled.

"Forgive me if I offended," he urged. "I spoke in good will. I wish to be thy friend."

Moussa, in spite of himself, was mollified. Granott was a good man, despite the disability of being an Infidel. "Come again when God wills it," he intoned, the majestic host. "I will be thy friend. But," he warned firmly, "I will not use thy machines."

4. IPE

There was a very useful spring flowing just east of the village. Here girls and women came with tall jars balanced on their heads, to get household water, to meet and gossip a little. Overflowing its stone cup, it went trickling down the hillside, pausing to form a pool in which village laundry was done, and then gradually losing itself in the hungry earth of the vineyards.

Yusif, his single garment flapping around bare brown shins, paused with an air of conscious superiority to watch some of the girls washing clothes. His lip curled a trifle, as befitted a male, a great warrior, and a son of the mukhtar. The fact that he was not the eldest son, Yusif considered to be a mistake on the part of Allah, who, doubtless, would presently correct His error.

He took a drink of water, which, being below the scene of laundering, tasted rather of old sweat and dirt; but Yusif was not particular. Wiping his mouth, he swaggered closer to cast a critical eye upon the labor. Jasmin was there, and her cousin Nejmi, and plump Shuhda and bold Amira, both sisters of Yusif's friends, and that impudent Katan, who failed to pay Yusif the respect he felt to be his due. He frowned upon them all impartially, and made a great show of watching to see if they were doing a good job of it. Not that he cared a twig whether his clothes were clean or not, but it was good to keep a firm hand upon females, or they might become lazy.

They had finished rubbing wood ashes and clay into the soiled garments, and most of these lay in the pool soaking. Jasmin and Nejmi had each taken a piece and begun to beat it with a heavy stick of wood, forcing ashes, clay, and dirt all out at once. Yusif felt that a comment was required.

"You are not working very hard," he told his half sister. "My father the Mukhtar would not like his daughter to be idle."

One never knew quite how Jasmin would react to this sort of remark. Sometimes she laughed. Sometimes —especially if her parents were not around—she would turn on him with a smart slap which at once outraged Yusif's dignity and increased his respect for her. Today, it seemed, she was at her most irritating— which meant that she was treating him as if he were a foolish child. This was much worse than being slapped. She was simply ignoring him! Infuriated, he hopped up and down and shouted at her in a shrill voice that reminded Jasmin irresistibly of his grandfather.

"Lazy!" he jeered. "Work harder, lazy female!"

Jasmin paused and glanced at Katan. "I think the flies will be especially bad this year," she observed. "Already I think I hear the loud and empty buzzing of one who is no doubt too young and foolish to know that if a fly is very annoying I am likely to slap it."

The other girls giggled. That Jasmin! It was true that she had a most extraordinary habit of attacking flies instead of ignoring them. And she also had a quick and daring tongue when she wished. She would make life lively for a husband some day—and for Yusif at once, if he was not careful.

"Go on, slap it!" urged Katan hopefully.

Yusif bristled, his dignity offended. Then he looked pleased, for he had found a clever retort.

"Foolish females forget that a fly may bite," he said, his round face split by a grin of frank admiration for himself.

Jasmin grinned back. She rather enjoyed Yusif when she was not wanting to drown him. He could be an engaging little devil—taken in small doses. "Why are you not in school?" she demanded, taking the offensive.

He looked lofty. "I do not choose to be. It bores me. And Mahmoud is dull, even though he is a holy man. For myself, I have no desire to be an imam or even a good man. I shall be a great warrior, and have already slain a hundred Yahud barehanded. Warriors have no need to learn stupid things like reading."

This was received with soprano derision from most of the girls, but by looks of pure hatred from Jasmin and Katan. Anyone who had the opportunity to learn things and rejected it deserved to be jabbed by a thousand devils for a thousand years! Jasmin's voice became waspish.

"And have you informed our father the Mukhtar of this decision?" she demanded tartly. "I am sure he would be most interested, oh small and ignorant half brother."

Yusif shifted his bare feet, feeling suddenly at an unfair disadvantage. How had he managed to lose the whip hand? "I shall discuss it with him—some day," he evaded airily. "I think you are not working hard enough, oh lazy one."

They glared at each other. Jasmin, whose back was aching from the bending and pounding, seriously considered the choice of several possible answers. There would be consequences perhaps—but it might be worth it . . . She grabbed Yusif and pitched him bodily into the pool.

He climbed out raging. He might tolerate Jasmin's impudence once in a while, but this was going much too far! It was an assault against his dignity! All the girls were laughing at him! Even Katan!

"You— You—" He sputtered, fishing for the worst insult in the world. He found it. "Female!" he howled. "You *females!* Female, *female,* FEMALE!" And he hurled himself, a dripping figure of vengeance, at the cluster of giggling girls, tore through them, and went for Jasmin with fists, feet, fingernails, and teeth.

But before he had got in even one really good blow, he found himself lifted into the air by the scruff of his wet garment and dangled there. Twisting, he discovered that it was his oldest half brother Ahmed, on his way back from fields or vineyard. "Let me go!" he bawled. "Female! Kus emmek!" he added balefully.

Ahmed cuffed him lightly. Since Ahmed was large and burly and fully grown, his idea of a light cuff was not the same as Yusif's. "Stop that," said Ahmed, a young man of few words. "Run away," he added economically, placing him on his feet again.

Yusif, holding the place where he had been cuffed, hesitated only briefly. It was true that he was a great warrior, or would be in a few weeks when he grew up, but surely there were sensible limits to heroism? Like the Arab armies before him, he decided that there was great wisdom in knowing when one had had enough. With a cheeky and philosophical grin, he obeyed.

Ahmed looked down at his sister, who was favoring him with her own peculiarly shining smile, like the golden flame of an oil lamp. It was a rare smile, kept for special occasions, not to be confused with an everyday smile or chuckle. He smiled back. He did not in the least understand Jasmin, or even try. But he loved her very much; even more than he did his brothers. This was odd, Jasmin being only a female, but there it was. Ahmed never worried about such things: he simply accepted them. The only things permitted to worry him were things concerning crops or land.

He frowned. He walked on, forgetting what he was going to say to Jasmin, or even that she was there. The girls stared after him for a moment, Amira with a small sigh, for she thought Ahmed wonderful and he never even *noticed* her. "What's the matter with him, Jasmin?" she asked as the girls turned back to their work.

Jasmin looked surprised. She had thought it perfectly obvious. "He's thinking about the harvest, of course. What else would he be thinking about the day before we begin reaping the wheat?" She gave an extra hard slap at the soaked tob on the rock, partly because it was Khalil's and partly just to let off steam. "Kus emmek," she whispered, but very much under her breath.

Bab-il-Howa was a beehive the next morning, well before Mahmoud's clear voice called the morning prayer. *"La Ilaha illa-Allah:* There is no God but God." Facing east, they went through the ritual: a serious one, called five times daily, never to be omitted or skimped—although it was just possible that minds regrettably wandered now and again. Ahmed's did so this morning. It was the crops. The moment prayers were over, he jumped to his feet, grabbed a handful of dried figs and olives, and drifted worriedly out of the house.

Even Kbeer Abou partook of wheat harvest—in his own way, which consisted primarily of wandering around telling everyone how much better the crops were in his day. On this score, Ahmed feared sorrowfully that he might be right. Even within his own young memory crops seemed to be getting poorer each year. Was Allah displeased about something? It seemed probable—but Ahmed couldn't help wondering now and again whether it might help if only he could plow more deeply and if there were more rain . . .

Munching his own casual breakfast, Khalil joined Selim just outside the gate, grinning at him comfortably. They needed no particular greeting: they frequently thought in each other's minds. By tacit consent they stayed clear of Hassoun and Ali and their crowd, who, being young men, were choosy about admitting boys to their select group. Selim in particular bore this deprivation with remarkable cheerfulness. He disliked Hassoun profoundly, considering him a braggart, a bully, a snake, and quite probably a coward. Moreover, he noted indignantly, he disliked the way he was looking at Jasmin as she danced by with Shuhda. It lacked respect.

Selim nudged Khalil. "Tell Jasmin to veil herself," he suggested, his voice oddly sharp.

Khalil needed no second hint. "Jasmin!" he roared. "Ipe!"

Jasmin set her lips with annoyance and tossed her head, but she pulled one long end of her veil across the lower half of her face. Hassoun's look had made her feel very strange, and somehow exposed, as if she hadn't got all her clothes on. For the first time she began to see some merit in veils.

Shuhda, already properly veiled, was lagging a little,

shifting the weight of her chunky baby brother to the other arm. It had been easier when he was small enough to carry in a sling on her back, as Hayat was carrying her baby, but this one was too big for that, now. He had to be tucked under an arm, with most of the weight resting on Shuhda's hip. The baby made no objection, being used to that means of travel, but Shuhda was getting tired.

"I'll carry him the rest of the way," offered Jasmin, and took the burden.

Shuhda gave a sigh of relief as they toiled along the hillside, to the field beyond the spring, reaching eastward, over a shoulder of the hill, to the threshing stone and the boundary of the village land. The sun was already searingly hot, and the baby was indeed heavy.

"I will thank Allah if he learns to walk early," said Shuhda. "Jasmin, did you notice Hassoun looking at you?" She giggled plumply. "Do you think he might ask your father for you? What marriage price will you have? Probably it will be too high for him to pay, since you are the Mukhtar's daughter, and pretty besides, even though you're much too skinny."

Jasmin's face flushed under its half veil. She didn't like Hassoun at all, even though most of her friends considered him so handsome. But his eyes were cruel—not at all like Selim's—and anyway, she didn't want to think about marriage yet, not for a long long time. This was unnatural, she knew, and it made her feel like some queer thing pretending to be a human girl.

She lifted slim shoulders restlessly as if to shake off an invisible burden.

"I'm too young," she murmured.

Shuhda stared. "Don't be silly, Jasmin; every girl thinks about marriage! Especially to Hassoun, who is quite the best-looking man anyone ever saw, and just twenty, which is a perfect age, not too old. Would you rather be second wife to an old man, like Tewfid or Ismail? Besides, you aren't so very young, Jasmin. You're already twelve, and my sisters married at thirteen. Still," she conceded hopefully, "you *are* younger than I, and *very* skinny. Perhaps Hassoun will ask for me instead."

"Oh, I *do* hope so!" said Jasmin in tones of utter sincerity that would have infuriated that very egotistical young man.

They had reached a small grove by the field, now, and Jasmin deposited the baby among the others, a crop of them hanging in little bags from the low branches of scrub oaks. And she made a point of avoiding places where Hassoun was working.

Khalil and Selim worked together in easy silence. Khalil grabbed a handful of stalks, cut them neatly near the roots with his small sickle, and tossed them in a pile for the smaller children to load on donkeys. He paused a moment staring at nothing. Selim (who, having no sickle, merely pulled up the wheat by the roots) looked questioning.

"Nothing," said Khalil, meaning that he was thinking of the Yahud again. Selim tugged at a determined clump of wheat until it came out, and then smiled. Then he forgot what he had been about to say, and stared out over the valley. Katan, near the threshing floor, squealed with excitement. In a moment the entire village had dropped whatever it was doing and stood watching.

Along the valley floor, winding along the crazy road, was a small caravan of assorted vehicles. Trucks were piled with lumber, machines, boxes; a tractor lurched just behind a jeep, and in an open truck, crowded together and singing, were some thirty or more Yahud, all wearing pointed cloth caps and khaki shorts with unbelievably long brown or black legs stretching beneath.

They reached the base of the hill. They passed beneath Bab-il-Howa, beneath the fields, waving and calling "Shalom!" to the transfixed villagers. And they pulled to a halt just beyond, at the edge of the narrow Jordan, not a mile from the Arab village.

Presently they were swarming along the foot of the hill, apparently engaged in setting up housekeeping then and there, and perhaps just planting a crop or two while they were about it. They were in and out of the trucks, hauling, measuring, shouting, unloading, digging, laughing, laying out a road and building-sites, putting up tents. They seemed to think nothing at all of settling in overnight. To people whose village had apparently grown where it was since the creation of the world, it seemed quite staggering and just a little shocking.

Then Jasmin's voice rang out, clear in the astonished silence.

"Look! Look, Shuhda; look everybody, look! Some of them—with their legs all bare—are WOMEN!"

Khalil felt himself blushing equally for the brazen Yahud and for his almost equally shameless sister. "Jasmin!" he roared, scandalized. "IPE!"

5. WAGGING TONGUES

Never had Bab-il-Howa found so much enthusiasm for work on its eastern boundaries! When the wheat harvest was over, there were just as many helping with the threshing. The sheaves were spread in a circular heap on the threshing floor—really just a large level place on the shoulder of the hill. All of the hooved village animals—oxen, donkeys, cattle—were fastened together in a line and driven around and around treading the yellow wheat. Now and then they would stop, and change directions; and men would turn the heap with wide wooden pitchforks, tossing it high into the wind so that the chaff blew away while the grain rained back down to earth.

It was the busiest season, and not the most pleasant, for the hot wind called *khamsin* blew from the desert, laden with fine dust. There was no time or energy to spare for staring—but they spared it. The work was done, somehow, with all eyes fixed eastward and downward, toward the *kibbutz* visibly growing at the bottom of the hill.

They did things so quickly, these Yahud! No decent deliberation at all. Almost overnight a large wooden building went up, in which, it was rumored with awe, they all cooked and ate together, and did wild singing and dancing in the evenings. There were also large, evil-looking machines (fascinating to Khalil, who managed to graze his goats within sight of them nearly every day) which simply tore rocks and shrubs from the earth, and another which plowed it magically. This was quite probably against the will of Allah, who must have wanted those things there or He would not have put them there in the first place. Kbeer Abou gleefully predicted divine vengeance, preferably in the form of thunderbolts, and was very much annoyed when days went by and nothing of the sort happened. Perhaps, he suggested (but not in Moussa's hearing) Allah wished the village to act for Him?

He didn't get much response. Just now resentment was nearly eclipsed by curiosity. Men crowded the threshing place, and the roofs of certain houses which had a view over the curve of the hill. Women and girls were seized with a passion for cleanliness, gliding back and forth to the spring with water jars or dirty clothes just as often as they could possibly manage. This was the most exciting thing that had happened in generations.

Presently smaller buildings—flimsy things of sheets of light wood—went up. There was a long sleeping-house where females went in and out—and while the

males were still getting along with tents, too! Then
sheds appeared where the machines lived, and then
more sheds, and cows and sheep and chickens to fill
them. A very young man with unlikely yellow hair
brooded over the soil, pacing and digging and feeling
it nearly up to the border on top. Ahmed watched him
with interest. Was it possible that a Yahudi might care
for the land as he did?

But always, while plowing and planting, building or
resting, the Yahud were on guard. Each one—even the
females—always had a rifle within reach, and at night
they patroled their land and also the border above. It
was even said that girls went on patrol as well as men,
but that was a little *too* much to swallow.

Still, it did look as if the Yahud meant to be amiable
but not to meddle. The soldiers down the valley contented themselves with keeping an eye on the border,
the new neighbors merely called or waved cheerfully
from a distance now and then. Moussa began to relax
and to forget the threat of change. His people had forgotten their panic. They no longer talked of escaping
to Lebanon, but instead spoke pityingly of the fools
who had done so, and now were barred from returning
to their homes. This, surely, was very unfair of the
Yahud! A man had a right to his home, and laws, patrols, barbed wire were no answer to that right.

They were not altogether a barrier to it, either.
Every night men trickled through, in one direction or
the other. Everyone knew it. Some of them even came

through Bab-il-Howa. Moussa deliberately closed his
eyes to this knowledge. No harm was being done. He
did not believe for a moment that the Yahud would
bother to drive them from the village even should they
find out, which was doubtful.

In any case, he had his hands full. Slowly Bab-il-
Howa was dividing itself into two camps of opinion.
The humiliation of defeat had bitten very deeply with
some men, and the sight of a Yahud settlement less
than a mile away, flaunting itself at them, brought
forth waves of venom. And on the other hand were
those with rather more interest and curiosity than
Moussa cared to see.

Jasmin, for one, had far more to say on the subject
than she ought. It consisted largely of questions. Embarrassing ones, mostly, having to do with why Yahud
girls went around with practically nothing on, and
their arms and legs all showing, and some with short
hair; and whether Allah punished them for it, and if
not, why not; and whether there were different rules
for Arab and Yahud women, and if so, why? And why
didn't the men beat them? Did they *approve?* And if so,
how could such a thing be?

The other members of her family regarded her with
varying degrees of astonishment and misgiving. She reminded them of a djinni bottle with the stopper suddenly removed and this spate of curiosity pouring forth
instead of the djinni . . . And on such a subject!

"Ipe!" Moussa thundered on a hot evening, tired

and therefore short-tempered from tending several oxen stricken with an illness. Moussa had a healing power with animals, which was much in demand. "Silence, my daughter! It is shameful for a girl even to think about such indecent matters!"

Jasmin subsided, but her eyes turned, brooding, to the eastern edge of the flat roof, where blue dusk was swiftly darkening and an orange glimmer showed from the kibbutz. Zubaida watched her apprehensively. Moussa, under the impression that he had settled this matter once and for all, studied her slender silhouette as she turned back to the wheat she was grinding. It was high time he thought about picking a husband for her. She would soon be old enough, and marriage would settle her down and give her new responsibilities, and take her mind off unhealthy things.

He went on watching her, not without pride. She was worth a very high bride-price, his Jasmin, surely the loveliest girl in the village, whatever his doting brother-in-law Rashid might say about his own Nejmi. Nejmi was overblown, lacking the delicate piquancy of Jasmin, whose short straight nose was like her mother's. So were the eyes, widely-set, shadowed with lashes like heavy curved fans. Thick black braids—almost blue-black—hung heavily over her hips, the waving ends touching the floor as she knelt to her work. To be sure, her figure was still slight and childish, but she was young yet. A husband would fatten her up soon enough, provided he didn't work her too hard, and

Moussa intended to pick the man very carefully indeed. And in addition to all her other assets, he decided comfortably but quite mistakenly, she was a docile and obedient girl at heart: modest, humble, easily managed.

Night had fallen, and a cool breeze curled over the hilltops from the sea. Moussa began considering prospective bridegrooms. The selection wasn't wide. The lucky man must be able to pay the bride-price, and must be of good character, and a kind nature, preferably neither very old nor very young . . . Hassoun had given him a hint the other day, but Moussa was not certain Hassoun would make Jasmin happy. Young, unstable, and inclined to kick animals for no reason than to express his bad temper. Ismail might be a better choice. He was a solid, steady, dependable man, not yet forty, with only one wife, two having died this last year. Yes, if Ismail could pay the *mahr,* he should make a good husband for Jasmin. She would be happy with him. It wasn't many fathers who were so deeply concerned over the happiness of a mere daughter, but Moussa cared very much indeed. Jasmin was his flower-child, whom he would not have exchanged even for another son!

Khalil found his twin nearly unbearable these days. It wasn't that she kept on asking those shameless questions, for she didn't. Not since Father had put his foot down. It was, rather, what she didn't say. It was those eyes, that looked so demurely at everyone else, and so challengingly at him. There was a devil asleep behind Jasmin's eyes. Khalil had known it for a long time, though no one else seemed to have noticed. And he had an uncomfortable feeling that it was beginning to wake up.

At the end of threshing, he just happened accidentally to be on the eastern side of the village, elaborately not watching the Yahud kibbutz, when he noticed a slim figure on the threshing-floor, shapeless kaftan blowing loosely in the wind. It was Jasmin, and she was making no pretense at not watching the briefly-clad girls below.

Khalil frowned. "Thy thoughts, oh my sister, would not be pleasing to Allah," he challenged.

Jasmin glanced at him, innocent and artless. "I have said nothing, oh my brother," she murmured, every word a taunt.

"I spoke of your thoughts. They are unbecoming a female, and you needn't try to fool me, Jasmin; I know."

She clasped her hands behind her and regarded him with the devil just a trifle more in evidence. "But I cannot help my thoughts," she pointed out, sweetly reasonable. "Since they exist, perhaps Allah wills them."

Khalil was doubly shocked because he had occasionally entertained the same sort of idea himself. "That's wicked blasphemy!" he warned her sternly. "You'd

better pray for a meek heart, Jasmin, or you'll go to
Hell. What's more, no one will want to marry you."
He paused, having the impression that she had said
something but if so, she didn't repeat it. "Now go
home this minute or I'll tell Father."

She turned, but the meekness had become a very
thin shell indeed. It cracked. "Since when did Allah
make thee guardian of my thoughts, oh meddling
brother?" she asked, so softly that Khalil was not quite
sure he had heard correctly. He scowled after her as
she took to her heels and raced along the hillside like a
small girl who had been caught in mischief. Maskin!
Bedouine! Her thoughts doubtless came from Shaitan,
and he wished he had thought to tell her so. But with
Jasmin, he always thought of the best retorts too late.
Infuriating!

Jasmin skipped back to the spring feeling highly
elated. This feeling vanished abruptly when she saw
her mother and an assortment of aunts and cousins,
baskets of laundry on their heads, just approaching
from the village. Wallah! She was supposed to be there
helping Mother!

Repentant, Jasmin ran to meet them, cutting down
from the spring so that it might look as if she had
been there all along. But there was no avoiding
Aunt Basna's sharp eye and tongue. Aunt Basna's personality did not at all match her comfortable plump-
ness.

"Here at last, oh Jasmin?" she remarked acidly.

"How kind of thee! No doubt it is very pleasant to sit idle by the spring while thy mother works."

"Thy tongue is too harsh, Basna," protested Aunt Yemna mildly. "Jasmin is scatter-headed, to be sure, but she means no harm. Remember how flighty and odd Sarika was at that age? Jasmin is much the same. And yet—" Her voice took on just a shred of doubt. "Yet look what a good wife and mother Sarika has become . . ."

Aunt Sarika's dull eyes turned to regard her drearily. Jasmin repressed a shudder. It frightened her to be told she was like Aunt Sarika, who was a spiritless empty shell, as if something within had been slain or removed. If settling down meant *that*, Jasmin thought she might as well die altogether and be done with it. Suddenly subdued, she took the laundry basket from her mother, and made herself useful.

When she next began to listen, Aunt Basna was on another complaint. "—deliberately trying to corrupt our young, or why else did they build right there where we must see their sinful nakedness day and night?"

"Only if we crane our necks or go to the rooftops," pointed out Aunt Yemna with a dry chuckle. Aunt Basna ignored this and went on.

"Kbeer Abou has been right all along, Zubaida, and thy husband wrong. We should have fought to destroy the Yahud, and then this would never have happened."

"No doubt the prowess of Kbeer Abou and thy husband would have turned the tide of war?" suggested Zubaida sweetly. "If they felt so strongly, there was no one keeping them here by force."

"Thy husband forbade joining the army."

"Yet Jawad went anyway," Zubaida retorted. "It sometimes seems to me, Basna, that some people in this village are better at talk than at deeds."

Basna breathed heavily, and angry silence drifted across the pool, untouched by the splash and thud of washing. Jasmin and the other girls filtered into a separate group, working downstream from the women. Their low-voiced conversation quite naturally took up the same subject.

"My mother is right," announced Nejmi, glaring at her cousin Jasmin, whom she disliked.

"*You* would say so, of course," retorted Amira, her narrow face looking impish.

Jasmin giggled. Nejmi flushed angrily, and Shuhda's placid voice just prevented some sharp words.

"Of course, each of us believes her parents are right. Is not this always so?"

As a matter of fact, decided Jasmin, it wasn't. Not always. Her eyes met Amira's in a gleam of understanding that angered Nejmi more than ever. Why should Jasmin make common cause with Amira against her? It was offensive. "You will make very bad wives, both of you," she declared, producing the worst insult she could think of.

Again the glance of secret amusement, followed by

nods of shameless agreement. Amira, for one, intended to wrap her future husband as firmly around her finger as did Nejmi's mother. Jasmin went even further.

"I hope so," she agreed with enthusiasm. "Moreover, if I do not like him, I shall be so wicked that he will divorce me."

There was a shocked gasp at this. "You couldn't!" bleated Shuhda. "You would be disgraced, and your father shamed, and no one else would ever marry you at all! Then what would you do?"

Jasmin had never really thought about such a possibility. But now, to save face, she leaped into further recklessness. "I would run away and live with the Yahud," she declared brashly, and even Amira's eyes rounded.

Katan had been listening silently, her keen little mind grasping much more than anyone suspected. Now she spoke. "Would you marry a Yahudi, Jasmin?" she inquired with deep interest.

"Katan!" said three shocked voices, and then three pairs of eyes turned to stare at Jasmin with morbid curiosity. Jasmin refused to haul down her flag. She tossed her head so that her thick braid flapped heavily against her back. "Why not?" she brazened.

It was perhaps fortunate that Aunt Basna's sharp ear caught the word Yahud. It was certainly fortunate that she hadn't caught the rest of the conversation. "Ipe, girls," she barked from the pool uphill. "It is ipe even to *talk* about them."

Jasmin grinned at the others with a rather satisfying sense of her own wickedness. And just let them dare tell their mothers, warned her expression. Even Nejmi decided it wouldn't be worth it. They all bent demurely to their task.

6. the arrogant yahudi

Selim turned his dark head on the bed-mat, deep-set eyes still closed. Then he opened them, fully awake. It was not yet dawn, and the assorted lumps of his family still slept more or less noisily here and there on the flat roof. The dawn breeze had come, and the sky over Syrian hills was faintly gray. It would be some time before the sunrise call to prayer.

He rose quietly, unable to rest. Something had been going on last night, and this time it wasn't just the furtive sounds of a few Arabs on one side of the border who felt an urgent desire to be on the other side. This had involved distant gunfire and explosion and a blossom of flame in the valley and another on the eastern hill. Selim had awakened and watched and listened, feeling oddly that something menaced Bab-il-Howa.

Now he wandered down the worn stone steps that descended the outer wall, and stood irresolute in the silence of the still-dark street. The hill loomed blackly above, and Selim felt the presence of a spirit of violence crowded against it, encircling the valley. Did the armistices that had been signed not mean peace, then, after all? Or was it men like Kbeer Abou, beards wagging, spitting forth words of hatred and violence into willing ears like those of Hassoun and Ali . . . Selim sighed. He had always known that he lacked that most desirable virtue of Arab manhood: a warrior spirit. It wasn't that he was a coward, or at least he didn't think he was. But he never could seem to work himself up to the proper frame of mind. Fighting merely seemed silly and wasteful, and also quite likely to lead to the wrong solution.

It was getting lighter now. Women began to stir in the cool gray of not-yet-dawn, and to clatter up and down stairs. White light began to pour over the rims of the eastern hills, turning them the blue of wild hyacinth, while the western range glowed shadowed rose.

"La Ilaha illa-Allah!" The call came just as the molten-gold disk appeared. Selim faced eastward, and in his heart was more than the usual prayer. There was an urgent appeal for peace, for friendship, even for what seemed to him simple sanity.

And then through the bright hush of morning came a new, alien sound, and Selim stared down into the valley.

There was—not surprisingly—signs of unusual activity from the Yahud settlements and military post. There were soldiers where he had seen fire last night, and trucks and jeeps scattered outward toward various Arab villages in the encircling hills, their sounds ugly to the morning. One was already at the foot of the village road, crawling upward, and Selim stood still, chilled. This was not a friendly social call; not this time.

As the jeep passed him, he glimpsed two armed soldiers in the back seat, and a red-haired driver who must be the same friendly young man who had driven Captain Granott. He looked less amiable now, but his frown was as nothing to that of his passenger, a man whose skin looked too tight for his craggy face, whose expression seemed carved in harsh pain. Grim lines curved downward beside a thin mouth, and deep-set eyes brooded inward, hot and angry.

Something in Selim's chest clenched a fist. He followed the jeep upward very much against his will. He could always, oddly, taste people's thoughts and feelings, and this man left a bitterness in the very air. A cloud of it trailed behind the jeep, and Selim wished he were out on the hills with the goats. But he kept going, joining the other villagers, who had seen the nice Red-hair but not the officer, and who were, therefore, in a mood more interested than hostile.

This was quickly shattered. When Selim reached the parked jeep, talk had already started. The officer's voice rose sharp and staccato and accusing. Moussa stood in massive silence, radiating dignity and slow anger. Mahmoud was at his shoulder, his sons ranged behind him, his brothers and cousins backing them. Kbeer Abou was doubtless hiding somewhere, and,

Selim hadn't the faintest doubt, Jasmin was listening behind the mukhtar's wall.

At first the Yahudi's speech was fragmented from where Selim stood. "—border raids—cowardly attacks on our kibbutzim—outrageous violation of the armistices—will be stopped and punished, both marauders from over the border and local Arabs!" The voice was rising now, and every word clear in the thick and hostile silence. "What do you know about it, Mukhtar?"

Selim saw Khalil's dark face flush with anger. How dare this—this Yahudi—address Moussa as if he were a nobody, a member of a conquered and inferior race? Show of authority might instill some of the villagers with respect; Selim could see it on a few faces around him. But for Khalil, with his touchy and doubtful pride, it was disastrous.

Moussa was somehow managing to look down his nose at the tall officer, his face impassive. "Why do you ask me?" he demanded. "We know nothing. We were promised peace for peace, and have kept the agreement. Do ye now break it? What of Yahud honor? First," he went on, carrying the war into the enemy camp, "First ye come saying we must now have new laws, and water in pipes, instead of being left alone to live according to Allah, and now—"

"Yes, yes!" interrupted Major Schorr. "I've heard it all before! Innocent as newborn puppies, aren't you? Wouldn't know what a gun looks like, any of you, or how to start a fire or set a bomb?" This last was perfectly true, at any rate, but no one said so. All watched Moussa, who stared back coldly at the bellicose eyes.

If the mukhtar had any faint doubts about last night and the possible activities of Hassoun and Ali, he kept these doubts well below the surface of his thinking. His indignation was genuine and his anger great. "Do you accuse my village of these deeds?"

"Not yet." The major looked as if he regretted this. "We have no proof—yet. But marauders crossed the border near here, and Kfar Shalom was attacked, and I should be very much surprised if some of you were not involved." Hot bitterness burst its leash suddenly. "You ought to be wiped out, the whole cursed race of you! Treachery, betrayal, and cruelty are the only things you know; you make virtues of them! You lie through your smiles, while you stab in the back! You break every promise, violate every treaty, massacre women and children and mutilate their bodies like the savage barbarians that you are! My own wife and baby—" He stopped, mouth clamped shut on any further words. "Why should I believe anything you tell me?" he asked in the old controlled voice, as if the outburst had never happened.

"If you do not believe me," said Moussa, stiff with insulted pride, "then I cannot help it. You will believe what you choose."

The major grunted, glanced at his driver's open dismay, became slightly more human. "I shall," he said grimly enough. "You must understand, Mukhtar, that we are not in a position to believe you. We know valley Arabs have been helping in these vicious attacks, yet you all claim to be our friends. How can we believe any of you?"

"*I* do not claim to be thy friend," Moussa pointed out drily. "We wish nothing to do with ye, either in friendship or enmity. Thy suspicions are thine own affair."

The major stared. A faint softening of the corners of his mouth was certainly not a smile, but it was less a frown. "That," he said, equally dry, "is the most convincing thing you could have said. If you were lying, you would most likely be protesting your great love for us, with much swearing by Allah . . . Well, if you are in truth neutral, see that you stay that way. And keep an eye on your people," he added sharply, with a glance at Khalil's furious face. "We'll be keeping one on you— and I warn you, if you give us trouble, you will be packed up and moved, the entire village, to some spot well away from the borders. Understand? That's all, then. Moshe, see if you can back the jeep down this confounded stinking wadi of a road without going through a house on the way," he finished in Hebrew, as if Moussa and the villagers had ceased to exist.

Jasmin, peering cautiously through a crack in the high wooden gate, quaked at the smouldering anger emanating from her father, and at the black fury she saw in her twin. Life was not going to be very comfortable for a while, that was clear. Only Mahmoud, standing quietly in his religious garb of gray denim robe and round white turban, seemed more sorrowful than angry. Even Ahmed was upset, doubtless at the possibility of being removed from the land he loved. Jasmin scuttled hastily back into the house, not at all anxious to confront any of them just now.

The crowd scattered, muttering darkly. Moussa stalked off somewhere, to the hills, no doubt, which was where he went in times of stress. None cared to ask or follow. Others drifted, talking hotly, back to homes or tasks or the coffeehouse. Kbeer Abou at once appeared, hurling strings of bold abuse after the departing jeep.

"I think," said Hassoun, his large teeth bared in an ominous smile, "that that officer needs a long knife in his back."

"Hah!" approved Kbeer Abou, panting with enthusiasm. "Mashallah! And all the other Yahud as well! You will do it soon, Hassoun?"

"He will if the Yahudi is obliging enough to return here alone and unarmed and in his sleep," sneered Ali, who contrived to look like a fledgling vulture, scrawny and not yet feathered. "There are easier and safer ways. Rifles from ambush, or bombs in the jeep, which Syrian soldiers told me about. Then they would all die."

Khalil smiled, pleased. That would assuage his wounded self-esteem! Selim, still apart, moved his shoulders restlessly, hating to see his friend join this group.

"The driver, the one called Moshe, was no enemy to us," he protested, knowing it was useless. "He would be friends."

"He has blue eyes, has he not?" pointed out Kbeer Abou unanswerably. "Evil they are, and he tried very hard to put the spell on me, seeing at once that I am the true strength and spirit of this village, and not to be fooled by false smiles. But I was too clever for him!" he crowed, triumphant. "I stayed behind a blue door, which protected me, although I think the spell fell on Selim instead."

Jasmin, drawn irresistibly back to her spot behind the gate, made an impudent face at the old man and wished wholeheartedly that a curse *had* fallen on him. She liked that red-haired Yahudi, and she liked Selim even better. Selim glanced that way as if aware of her thoughts, glimpsed her face through the crack, and twinkled at her. When they were children and played together, he used to think it a pity Jasmin wasn't a boy. Now, for some reason, he began to feel very glad that she wasn't. In response to his twinkle, joy fell about Jasmin in sparkling bits and the radiance of her special smile came right through the crack, startling Selim.

Then the brief moment of lightness fell away, for the small group on the road had gathered closer.

"We will think of something," Hassoun was saying, looking masterful and efficient. "Are you with us, Khalil?"

And Khalil, still raging inwardly, nodded. These arrogant Yahud must be taught a lesson.

7. the magic powder

Summer days grew hotter, and the emerald hills had long faded to amber and topaz. Water was jealously conserved now, for cisterns were nearly empty, and the spring flowed less generously; and although there was always the Jordan down in the valley, it was a time-consuming trip for women and girls balancing water jars on their heads, who had plenty of other work to keep them busy. Men could not be expected to work every day as though it were harvest.

("Why not?" wondered Jasmin, experimentally subversive. "Ipe!" said her mother.)

Ahmed was wrapped up in his precious vineyard. He built thorny protective hedges around, and even cleared stones from the ground, and scratched little channels for the spring water to flow near the roots. Kbeer Abou said he was inviting the wrath of Allah, who had put those stones there because He wanted them there. Even Moussa observed tolerantly that Ahmed made himself a prisoner to the land, which was surely reversing the order of things.

"It is part of man's dignity that he be free not to work if he choose," he pointed out. "Do you see me a slave to such things?"

"Aye," grunted Ahmed. "Sick animals," he added by way of complete explanation.

His father's face lowered between black beard and brows for an instant, then relaxed into a smile. It was true. Let an animal in the entire village be ailing, and Moussa would be with it until it got better or died. Surprisingly often it got well, because of his strange healing gift . . . although his powers had not been strong enough to save Yusif's mother and his three children two years ago. Moussa tried never to think of them. Instead, he looked at the shy sweetness of Hayat with her baby daughter, and humbly thanked Allah for his mercies.

A hot desert wind gusted across the roof where the family sat in the starry dark. Below, other families could be seen on other rooftops. Over the ridge of the hill and downward, the yellow lamps of Kfar Shalom shone in narrow lines at window edges and in small blobs here and there as patrols made their rounds. The Yahud clearly preferred to suffer the heat indoors rather than make themselves illuminated targets for any stray Arab with an unfriendly turn of mind.

In this, Khalil told himself with a curl of his wide mouth, they were undoubtedly wise. There must be a great many Arabs who felt as he did. He blazed inside every time he remembered Major Schorr. And for that matter, they were all unbearably sure of their own superiority. Even their friendliness held the galling stamp of kindness, of condescension. Intolerable! Not to be endured! What was Father about that he sat and did nothing? Didn't he care? Or did he think the Yahud would vanish if ignored long enough? And Selim seemed to have no pride at all. Only Hassoun and his friends had the right viewpoint about this matter. Getting up, Khalil went down into the darkened street to find them.

Jasmin stared resentfully after the descending whitish smudge of his khaffiya. She knew what he was thinking: she usually did. And she most passionately disagreed. It was true that that officer had been horrid and wicked, and it must be true that they were all a *little* wicked considering that the females went around half-naked . . . but oh, what a fascination they were! They had put interest and excitement into the dreary routine of village life, and Jasmin did hope that they would not be driven away.

But she did not think things could be very comfortable for them. The border seemed a very active place lately. Not all the Yahud in the valley were enough to patrol all of it, and there was more excitement here now than during the war itself. And every time there was a really bad raid or sabotage, the Yahud tightened restrictions, or perhaps there was another warning visit from an officer. Even shepherd boys taking their flocks down the valley for better pasture were sometimes given very close scrutiny or were even stopped and questioned.

Voices sounded from below, and presently Hayat's Uncle Ismail appeared, heavy jowls sagging a little beneath his skimpy beard in the light of the small oil lamp. "Men to see thee, oh Mukhtar," he said, and tactfully but reluctantly drifted back down the stairs.

"May Allah lengthen thy days," said one of the visitors perfunctorily.

"The blessing be on thee," Moussa replied with considerable reserve. What did they want, these strangers?

He was not left long in doubt. "We are Syrian," announced one who called himself al-Zaim. "We come to ask what you are doing for the Arab cause."

"Minding my own business," said Moussa promptly. "Why are ye not doing likewise?"

They looked at one another doubtfully, not having run into anything quite like this before. "We are serving the Grand Mufti," announced Gammel pompously.

This was a mistake, of course, Moussa's opinion of that gentleman being exceedingly low. He looked even more massive than usual, and the assorted arguments used on him for the next half hour were as raindrops beating against a boulder.

"Our job this time is merely to talk to important people and to spy out weak defenses," explained Gammel. "Next trip we will arrange for Arabs living inside this border to steal government secrets. This is being arranged all the time. You would be useful at it."

"I know no government secrets," observed Moussa.

"Of course not," agreed al-Zaim, giving Gammel a sharp elbow. "There are other useful things you can do, being here at the border. Thy village can be as a door to us, to come in and out at will. Shall we destroy the accursed Yahud village down the hill? Let us know how many armed men and tanks and machine guns they have. You can also tell us if any Arabs are friendly to any Yahud, so that we may punish them for being traitors. Two Arab villages have already been punished for that sin. Have you guns and ammunition? How many men can you . . ." It began to occur to al-Zaim that he was failing to produce the slightest hint of enthusiasm—or even co-operation—from his host. His voice trailed off into puzzled silence.

"No," said Moussa when it seemed clear that the speech had at last wilted from lack of nourishment.

"No?" They couldn't quite believe their ears.

"No," Moussa repeated, sounding pained at their inability to understand plain Arabic. "I told thee, I mind my own village. I want no trouble and I make none. Find others to do thy spying and shooting. But not," he added, rumbling like thunder, *"not* from my village."

"Art thou friend to the cursed Yahud, may pigs defile their graves?" exploded Gammel. "He who is not their enemy is their friend, and we know how to treat Yahud-lovers! We will burn thy village, and—"

"I think Allah has taken thy wits," Moussa told him with disconcerting kindness. "You cannot burn a village of stone. Moreover, it will not help Allah's cause if you should attack other True Believers. If I should do as you wish, we should at once be driven from our village, and that would do you no good, nor your masters, nor Allah. I advise you to go about your own affairs, which I am sure must need all your attention, and leave me in peace."

And he ushered his annoyed and perplexed guests down the stairs and out of the village while his wives and daughter giggled softly in the far corner of the roof.

Jawad returned one night soon after that, limping from his trip back over the Syrian hills, and soured at all the world. Moussa received him in grim silence, not only because Jawad was a chronic troublemaker but also because he had broken the laws in returning, and the whole village might have to suffer for it. But Bab-il-Howa was Jawad's home, and a man had a right to go home, and Moussa had a responsibility to all his people —even Jawad. So he said nothing and resolved to lie if the Yahud should ask.

Jawad had little enough to say to Moussa, but he talked at great length to all others who would listen. This included Kbeer Abou, Hassoun, Ali, and now Khalil.

"The Arab armies and the Mufti were liars," he grumbled. "They said we would annihilate them in two weeks. Instead, the cowards allowed themselves to be beaten. But the Yahud are great rogues. They do not fight fairly, for one thing. They did not wait for dawn to attack, but began fighting at any time of day or night, when we were not expecting it. Moreover, they must have had devils helping them, for how else could small numbers of them have beaten large numbers of us, who are the greatest fighters on earth?

"And now," he went on, his grievance mounting, "they are trying to prevent us from coming back to our homes! They arrest those who are caught trying, and torture and imprison them; and they are wiping out entire villages! They plan to massacre us all and take our property for themselves."

Common sense asserted itself in Khalil's mind briefly and tentatively. "How do you know this?" he asked, curious.

Jawad scowled at him. "Everyone knows," he said so masterfully that any faint doubt died at once. After all, it was just what they had been telling each other all along, now verified. Kbeer Abou went off on a long tirade. Hassoun fingered his knife thoughtfully. Ali thrust his head forward on its skinny neck.

"That cursed officer has set the Yahud village down there to spy on us and perhaps shoot us from ambush," he pointed out. "It is they who will want to take our land. Shall we not do something first?"

"Aye!" squealed Kbeer Abou. "Slay them all!"

Ali grinned at Khalil companionably, his yellow teeth as offensive as always, and Khalil liked him no better than he had ever done—but there was a bond between them now.

"How can we do it?" asked Ali. "They are yellow dogs, but not sheep who will walk under our knives. They stand watch at night, and if one tries to shoot them in the dark, they shoot back. And they have very good luck at hitting things," he complained with an air of one who had personal experience in this matter. Khalil looked at him speculatively. How much did Father know of all this? He was usually aware of everything that happened in Bab-il-Howa. Did his silence now mean that he didn't know or that he approved unofficially, even though he forbade them all to commit any act against the Yahud?

On the whole, this seemed likely, thought Khalil, and turned his attention back to the discussion with a happier conscience. Father didn't *want* to know; therefore Khalil wasn't really deceiving him.

"We must be subtle and clever and tricky," Hassoun was saying.

"We need the magic powder that goes bang!" declared Kbeer Abou.

"Dynamite?" Jawad looked important. "I know all about dynamite and bombs, and perhaps I could get some of the powder. But it is a dangerous trip back over the border and across the hills. Someone must go with me."

"Khalil?" suggested Ali, but Hassoun shook his head decisively.

"Moussa would notice at once if his son is missing,

thou fool!" he pointed out contemptuously. "Ali will
go. And there must be no talk of this!"

He turned to the old man in a manner that very
much lacked the respect Kbeer Abou felt to be his
due. "Do you hear that, oh father of many words?"
he demanded. *"No talk!* Not to anyone, and especially
Moussa. And no mysterious hints, either, or all will
be ruined, and thy son-in-law will be very angry at
thee indeed."

Khalil had no impulse to stand up for the indignantly fuming Kbeer Abou. What Hassoun had said
was true.

And so for two or three days thereafter, Jawad and
Ali were not seen in the village. If Moussa noticed, he
said nothing; and Khalil was more sure than ever that
he simply preferred not to know. After all, he was also
angered, and must certainly want a blow struck for
Arab pride.

Khalil saw little of Selim these days, since he did not
like Khalil's new friends, and Khalil knew it. He added
this to the score against the Yahud.

On a dry, hot morning, Khalil was going to the fold
when Ali appeared, beckoning urgently. Hoping that
Father would not catch him neglecting the goats,
Khalil followed down the pungent street to the mean
and smelly home of Jawad, where he and Hassoun
waited. By tacit agreement, Kbeer Abou was not
there.

"We have the magic powder, the dynamite," announced Jawad proudly. "And also the blessing of our Syrian brothers. Tomorrow, or perhaps the next day, the Yahud village will be no more."

Khalil looked respectfully at the swathed bundle on the floor. "Is that it?" he demanded with eager curiosity. "What does it look like? What is it made of? What makes it work? How do you know it won't go bang too soon and destroy our village instead of the Yahud one?"

"No fear!" crowed Jawad, his dark sagging cheeks lifting in a smug grin. "I know all about it, and how to work it. It is magic, I say, and will not go bang until I tell it to. All we need do is hide it in the Yahud village and tell it to go bang at midnight."

Khalil frowned a little. It was true that he knew nothing about dynamite, but this did not sound right: not logical. Surely modern magic of the West worked on different principles from the old-fashioned kind? One, he had thought, needed to *do* something, like pulling a trigger or lighting a fire, before it worked. But Jawad seemed very positive, and Khalil was not sure enough to risk mockery from these older men. And in any case, there was another problem to be thought about.

"How do we get it into the Yahud village?" he asked practically.

Apparently no one had thought of this. A blank silence was followed by a number of very silly ideas, none of which could possibly work. Khalil began to wonder about the intelligence of all three of his allies.

"I think," he said at last, and had to stand up and flap his aba before they would listen to a mere boy, "I think we must pay a visit to the village and hide it while we are there."

This shattering idea aroused much argument. It was beneath Arab pride. The Yahud would shoot them on sight. Besides, who would go first? But at last Hassoun took fire.

"It is very clever," he decided. "I had just thought of it, myself. We will go while Moussa is not looking, and tell the Yahudi mukhtar that we have come to seal a bond of great friendship, and drink their coffee, and tell them what love we feel for our new brothers. And it is well known that the foolish Yahud fall very easily into this kind of trap, and even sometimes think that the laws of hospitality apply to enemies and Unbelievers. And then, after we have gone, Bang! No more Yahud village."

This aspect of the matter had not occurred to Khalil. It made him feel uncomfortable. Surely it was one thing to make war on an enemy, and quite another to betray vowed friendship and hospitality? Moreover, he had never heard either Father or Mahmoud say that the laws of hospitality did not apply to Unbelievers. He began to wish he had never thought of the idea. But it was too late now.

"We will do it this afternoon," Hassoun was announcing, and they were deep in a discussion of how the dynamite should be hidden beneath their robes and then planted somewhere in the village.

"I fear I cannot go with thee," said Khalil awkwardly. They looked at him, eyes narrowed. "I must take the goats out," he explained. "If I do not, my father will want to know why."

"Oh, very well," agreed Jawad. "But be on your rooftop tonight so that you can see the Yahud village go bang. It will be a fine sight."

The family were all on the roof as usual that night, enjoying the cool of evening. Khalil kept a nervous eye and ear fixed in the direction of Kfar Shalom. But the moon sailed tranquilly across the spangled sky, and no roar, no burst of flame shattered the peace.

Jawad had bungled, decided Khalil at last, unsurprised; and was not quite sure whether he was sorry or relieved.

8. "shall a mukhtar be obeyed?"

The next morning five Yahud from the new kibbutz paid a visit to Bab-il-Howa. They wore shorts and clean blue shirts, which looked odd indeed beside the full *tob* and *aba* of the Arabs. Their hair—black, brown, and fair—was cropped short, and covered with the peaked cloth caps against the sun.

Moussa showed neither pleasure nor hostility. His deep-set eyes were wary, waiting. Khalil, suddenly uncomfortable, wished himself out with the goats.

"Salaam aleikum," said a burly man with curling brown hair. He seemed to be the leader, perhaps the mukhtar, by far the oldest, although he could not be much more than thirty.

"Salaam aleikum," replied Moussa formally, but he did not add, "Welcome."

"May Allah lengthen your days," the burly man went on firmly. "I am Avram Eshet, and these with me are Leo, Josef, Chaim, and Dan. I am leader of the new

village, which we call Kfar Shalom, Village of Peace.
We hope it will be so between us." He spoke Arabic
well, and Khalil found himself resenting this. They
thought themselves superior, no doubt, because they
could speak two languages.

Moussa bowed his head slightly. "What will be will
be," he said formally but without enthusiasm. "We
also wish peace." His tone indicated strongly that what
he meant was "We wish to be left in peace, so go
away."

Avram seemed not to perceive this. His eyes were
steady, a trifle challenging. "We come," he remarked
casually, "to return the visit of friendship paid by some
of thy people yesterday."

Moussa was startled, to say the least of it. His black
eyes flickered briefly and narrowed. He felt a surge of
anger. Either the Yahud or some of his own people
were deceiving him and it placed him in a very awkward position. Not caring to commit himself until he
knew more, he merely stared impassively at the lean
young faces before him and waited.

"We were happy to receive such a gesture of friendship, and to give hospitality," Avram went on. "We
wish to return it, and we wish also to ask whether thy
people left a bundle behind by accident or whether it
was meant as a gift of friendship."

There was something behind the mild voice that
caused Moussa to glance sharply at his visitors and then
swiftly around at the villagers who clustered around

the coffeehouse. It did not escape him that Ali, Hassoun, and Jawad were looking profoundly uncomfortable. Khalil's expression did escape him, because Khalil, with a sudden, urgent sense of responsibility, had gone to take the goats to pasture.

For all his stolidity, Moussa could draw swift and accurate conclusions. He did so now, and his anger began to turn from the Yahud and toward those of his village who had apparently tried to cause trouble.

"What is it that my people left?" he asked, and only a sharp ear could have heard the edge under the polite curiosity.

"It was a package of dynamite," replied Avram, equally polite. "It was left hidden behind some other things in our big eating-house. It is fortunate that we found it, for if it had accidentally exploded, I think Major Schorr, who is a suspicious man, might not have believed that it was an accident."

It was a clear warning. But it was tactfully delivered not as conqueror to conquered, but as mukhtar to mukhtar. Moussa's dark face tightened and his eyes looked through Avram for an instant. Then he met the clear gray eyes, and his head was high, and there was nothing behind his voice that could be read.

"If my people did make such a gift, it was very foolish, for it might be misunderstood," he said. "However, I think someone else must have left the package, for there has never been any dynamite in my village. You say you gave hospitality? Then you must accept mine. Come."

He led the way, not to his home, but into the coffee-house, straight and angry. He had been put into a humiliating position. Further, he was being forced to establish hospitable relationship, against his will. He would have something to say to certain people later.

He said it after the Yahud had left, when the villagers had been called together, and he stood before them, massive, formidable, blackly angry. "Am I mukhtar of this village or am I not?" he demanded.

The villagers regarded one another uneasily. Most of them, by now, had a fair idea of what had happened. "You are our mukhtar, oh Moussa," they agreed, that being a safe start. "May you live forever," a few voices added, hoping to pacify him.

Moussa was not pacified. "Shall a mukhtar be obeyed?" he asked grimly. "Or is there a new custom now? Did I or did I not pledge myself and my village to remain at peace with the Yahud? Has anyone heard me say that I wish to make war?"

"But that Yahudi officer said we are enemies," ventured Ali, since no one else seemed inclined to speak. "If we are enemies, shall we not act as such?"

He looked at his fellow-conspirators for support, but got none. Hassoun was looking straight ahead, stony-faced. Jawad tried to look shatteringly innocent and succeeded in looking completely guilty, while Kbeer Abou elaborately pretended to be somewhere else. Ali subsided, wilting under Moussa's wrath.

"Have the Yahud brought dynamite to Bab-il-Howa? Have they tried to commit violence against us?

Or have they only spoken discourteous words of enmity and suspicion? Shall we then make their suspicions true and give them reason to drive us forth from our homes? What shall I say to the officer if he tells me again that Arabs are treacherous dogs who hide a knife behind a smile? Ye have made his words true by violating hospitality—and hospitality which you yourselves asked! Vipers! Hyenas! Jackals! Moreover, ye put me under obligation to offer hospitality in return. I wished no communication with this Yahud village— but ye created a debt of treachery to be wiped out! Unclean pigs!"

He paused, looking over the crowd of abashed faces, daring them to answer. They shuffled uneasily. Then Kbeer Abou could no longer keep silent.

"It was not I," he protested in an aggrieved whine. "I was innocent, for they never told me of it; I, who am the true strength of this village. And besides, I would have had a much cleverer idea."

This started a chorus of protests, all shouting that they were innocent—mostly truthfully. "I will tell thee who it was!" shouted a voice from the back. "It was—"

"Nay, do not tell me!" interrupted Moussa. "If you tell me, I shall have to punish, and I do not wish to do that—this time. This is a warning. If there is any more violence attempted from this village, those men responsible shall leave, and may crawl their way back to Syria—" He looked hard at Jawad—"or anywhere else they please. If there are boys pretending to be men—"

and his eye fell on Hassoun and Ali—"they shall be well beaten to teach them obedience."

Hassoun flushed darkly. "And what of thine own family, oh Mukhtar?" he asked impudently.

Moussa glanced at Kbeer Abou, who glared back defiantly. It was a mean question, respect for the old being deeply ingrained in Arab thought. But Moussa was mukhtar, and had a greater responsibility than merely to the old. Moreover, his authority might be at stake.

He drew himself up. "I speak to my own family as well as to the rest of ye, oh son of insolence," he said, staring at Hassoun until the younger eyes fell, sullen. "I do not speak of wild and threatening words. To speak violence is not to commit it, and I do not punish for that—provided no injury is done to others."

There was a general murmur of approval. It was a good answer, both fair and clever. Everyone knew that Kbeer Abou would never do more than talk, and that Khalil had not actually helped to take the magic powder to the Yahud village.

They scattered about their own affairs, making the most of free speech, and bitterly berating Jawad either for his stupidity in failing to make the dynamite go bang, or in trying it at all. Moussa stamped up the hill to comfort himself with the patient trust of sick animals. He had no suspicion that his own son was involved.

The next few days were miserable ones for Khalil. He was at war with himself—which of course meant at war with all the world as well. A host of devils were in his mind, tearing it one way and then another. He hated himself for taking any part in such a dishonorable kind of plot—but then he hated the Yahud even more for being the cause of it—and this ended up with his wishing the plot had succeeded. He wished Father would scold him, even beat him, and clear the air, instead of acting as though he didn't even know Khalil had been mixed up in it. It never occurred to him that Moussa *didn't* know.

What with one thing and another, Khalil became quite unbearable, and he took it out mostly on Jasmin —who somehow offended him in much the same way the Yahud did. Moreover, she had got much worse since that first glimpse of the bare-legged Yahud women. She had learned how to lift a straight eyebrow or turn a shoulder with perfectly unspeakable contempt that no one saw but Khalil. And once when, goaded, he knocked her down for it, Father, misled, beat *him*.

It was a relief to everyone when Moussa sent him down the valley with the goats for several days grazing.

The day Khalil left, Selim returned from a similar trip, vaguely apprehensive over what might have been happening while he was gone. He led his herd past the kibbutz, noting that a new wooden building had been finished, and vegetables throve in neat rows in the garden, and faint green appeared over the newly sowed fields, with channels leading in from the river to water them. It was an astounding idea. Selim wondered if Ahmed knew about it. There were the beginnings of tiny trees on the slope of the hill above the living quarters, too. Selim stood on the flank of the hill below the threshing place, staring in wonder. It wasn't the machinery that fascinated him; it was the people. How did it feel, to be a Yahudi? What did the world look like through their eyes?

Someone stood on the threshing place above, also watching. It was Jasmin, silhouetted against the sky so that she looked thin and frail and infinitely vulnerable. A meager pile of sticks and dry dung had spilled out of her basket, and Selim knew with a sudden flash of insight that she always came this way for fuel, even though there was virtually none left here. And still she came, to watch the Yahud, risking scoldings for taking too long or bringing too little.

She threw him a swift glance as he climbed the small slope between them, questioning, at once pleading and trustful. But he was looking at her with the old friendly smile, as if he actually knew how she felt about things. "Do you find them interesting too?" he asked.

She nodded gravely. "They say the women are shameless, and it must be so, because look at them. But— But, *why?* Why do they dress and behave like that? Are things— Is it possible that among them such things are all right?"

Just the sort of thing he had been wondering—but from her prison of femaleness, she saw a different side. With sudden vividness, Selim saw it too. "I think it must be all right with them," he agreed slowly. "It's— astonishing—isn't it? That people have a whole different set of rightness and wrongness . . . Of course, not believing in Allah makes a difference," he added, but with questions still in his voice. They stared at each other with a sense of companionship that was rather a surprise to both of them. Then Jasmin stooped for her basket.

"I must go back," she murmured, flustered. "I— Salaam, Selim." And she hurried off, the basket swaying slightly atop the proud little head.

Selim stared after her, breathing the wistfulness she had left behind. Absently he gathered the straying goats. It must be very depressing to be a girl.

9. the jeep

Khalil sat and thought for the better part of two days, not even bothering to play the wooden flute which he carried tucked into his belt. Buazza the dog had to take most of the responsibility for the herd, running up now and then to thrust an anxious nose into his master's palm and whine. Khalil hardly noticed, busy circling on his endless wheel of shame and blame, nursing his grievance the more tenderly because he suspected that it wasn't altogether fair or reasonable.

And then the stocky figure of his cousin Alouf appeared, waved stolidly, and led his goats unhurriedly across to where Khalil sat.

Khalil was not displeased to have company, even though Alouf was not really a stimulating conversationalist. His long face wore the peaceful look of one who has never learned how to worry or even to think. His dullness might be a great comfort just now.

He stood regarding Khalil with simple pleasure. The mukhtar's son was younger than he, but terribly clever and altogether admirable. "Salaam," he said presently, looking as pleased as if he had just invented this satisfying form of greeting.

"Salaam," said Khalil.

"Thou art well?" Alouf went on gravely, in the ancient formal ritual of greeting which, having learned, he now used on all occasions.

"Very well, thanks be to Allah." Custom would have demanded this reply if Khalil had been suffering two broken legs and the plague, but his voice lacked conviction. "And thou?"

"Very well also. And are thy goats well?"

"Well indeed, by the grace of Allah; and thine?" Khalil began to wish for Selim, whose eyes would have sparkled with shared fun behind the still gravity of his face.

"Most well. Is thy dog well?" The ritual went on through everything Alouf could think of, even including the wooden flute. Alouf was nothing if not thorough. But at last he ran out of things to inquire about, and seated himself on the brown grass beside Khalil, at a loss for further conversation. The goats, well mingled, continued to graze, eating everything that had dared try to grow—grass, flowers, small plants, shrubs, and young trees—down to the roots and even the roots themselves. Khalil had noticed that it took years for anything to grow where goats had done much grazing. It was the way of goats, and therefore the will of Allah —but Khalil sometimes wondered why. It certainly made things more difficult.

He turned suddenly to Alouf. "What do you think of the Yahud?"

Alouf looked startled. His full lower lip drooped slightly as he strove to take in the question. No one had ever asked him such a thing before, and he was altogether at a loss.

"I do not know," he decided at last.

Patiently—for one must be patient with Alouf—Khalil tried to simplify the question. "Do you like them?"

Alouf looked baffled. "Which ones?" he asked, after considering this for a moment.

It was Khalil's turn to blink. Somehow he did not want to consider this point. "All of them," he persisted.

Alouf looked reproachful. "But I do not know all of them," he pointed out, confused.

Again Khalil shifted ground. "What of the ones you have seen? You were there when the soldiers came to our village, were you not?"

Alouf cast back into the dim fog of his memory. At last he nodded. "Oh yes, I remember. One had fire hair and the Evil Eye, but he was not evil. And the other was very angry because he was so sad."

"Sad!" echoed Khalil so violently that Alouf retreated into a startled silence.

Many long minutes passed while Khalil did some mental wrestling and Alouf watched him with concern.

"Do you hate the Yahud, Khalil?" he ventured presently.

Khalil nodded, glowering.

"Oh." More silence. "All of them? Have they harmed you, then?" he inquired with childlike innocence. "If they are evil and have harmed you," Alouf decided agreeably, "I will hate them too."

Had they harmed him? Major Schorr had been offensive in a way that harmed Arab pride. It was a genuine injury. As for the others, they— They— How could he explain to the simple-minded Alouf that they offended him by just existing? Alouf would not understand. Khalil was not sure he understood, either. Perhaps it was, then, not a good enough reason for hatred? Khalil did not relish the notion that perhaps he was being unreasonable. He frowned.

"Shall I hate them, too, Khalil?" repeated Alouf after a time.

Khalil shook his head slowly. "No. Let us wait and see."

Alouf nodded, perfectly satisfied. Presently he and his dog separated the flocks and drifted off, further down the valley. Khalil took another direction and settled down again, this time just between a deserted Arab village and another new Yahud one, right up on the Lebanon border. It was as energetic, as irritatingly efficient and self-confident as Kfar Shalom. Khalil began to study his own annoyance as well as the kibbutz. Why did he feel this way?

He found no answer, but asking the question had somehow taken the edge off of his bitterness. He decided to follow his own advice to Alouf: to wait and see. It occurred to him that he might be in danger, otherwise, of behaving like Kbeer Abou, whom he did not at all admire.

Feeling more at ease with the world, he started home at last. And at the edge of the valley floor, a few miles from Bab-il-Howa, he met Selim, also heading home. They smiled at each other, the rift between them as if it had never been, and walked on together.

They were making a leisurely way just along the foot of the parched hills when, around a curve and in the middle of the dusty road, they beheld a jeep, standing quite still and silent. From beneath it protruded a pair of long sandaled feet, twitching slightly in a way that suggested great effort. From the other side, a lean, khaki-shorted behind stuck out, also heaving now and then.

The boys regarded this scene with interest. The goats, unconcerned about such matters, proceeded to spread up the hill and around the jeep, and Khalil, his dark eyes alight with cryptic amusement, permitted them to do so. He and Selim glanced at each other and took up positions near the waggling behind, still and grave as two statues, their dark abas falling into frozen folds around them.

Presently Ibn Shaitan, the black goat, discovered the jeep. Being in a curious and aggressively sociable mood, he at once poked his horned head under it. *"Baaah?"* he demanded, loudly and inquiringly just as another goat gave the waving behind a friendly little butt.

The result was spectacular. The behind vanished under the jeep with one frantic wriggle, heaved briefly, and became a red head peering warily over a rifle barrel. On the other side, the sandals also turned into a head, this one lean and set, with a wave of black hair in the middle of the forehead.

Khalil and Selim continued to observe them gravely, unmoving, only their dark eyes brimming with amusement. And after an instant the freckled face under the red hair relaxed and grinned.

"Whew!" he exclaimed. *"Ain devar,* Leo. This is the first time I've ever been ambushed by goats," he explained in Arabic, crawling out from under the jeep. "You gave us a fright, my friends. And what is more," he discovered, looking closely at them, "you did it on purpose."

"Nay," protested Selim with a straight face. "Why should we do such a thing?"

"Because it amused you," he suggested, looking not sure whether it amused him or not. He looked hard at Selim and then Khalil, while Leo came around the jeep to join him. "I remember you," he said. "You are from Bab-il-Howa."

"And you are Mo-shee, who drives officers in the jeep," replied Selim.

"Not any more." Moshe made a relieved face. "Now I'm just a kibbutznik at Kfar Shalom with my other friends. Thank goodness!"

Khalil cocked his khaffiya. "You do not like driving the Major Schorr?" he hinted.

Moshe grinned engagingly. "Would anyone?" He paused, for Leo was talking in Hebrew, as his Arabic was limited. "Leo says I should explain about Major Schorr," he added with a shrug. "His family were all taken away and slain by some people called Nazis, and he came to Palestine and married, and then his wife and baby were also slain—uh—last year." He looked embarrassed. "It makes him bitter," he added.

Khalil and Selim considered this bit of information, each in his own way, without comment. Selim was filled with compassion for the unfortunate man. Khalil was far more interested in that fascinating jeep.

"Your machine," he asked, staring. "Is it ill?"

"Very ill," Moshe nodded, and then listened to another suggestion from Leo. "Perhaps you would like to help us fix it?"

There was nothing they would like better. The goats were abandoned to the care of the dogs, and soon there were four sets of feet and waggling behinds, in and under and around the disgruntled jeep, with Moshe explaining the workings of the monster to the enthralled Arab boys. An hour later it was running again, they were all liberally coated with oil and dust, and a kind of friendship had been established.

"Come visit us at Kfar Shalom when you can," invited Leo with a smile that made up for the peculiarity of his Arabic. Selim noticed that there were two layers to this Leo, almost as if he were in the process of shedding one skin like a snake, for a nicer one.

"We will come if Allah wills," he said tactfully, really meaning if Moussa wills, and rather doubting it.

"You will find more friends there," urged Moshe. "You will like them. There is Dan, who loves the land and growing things, and Josef who makes beautiful music, and Shari, who wishes to dig and find old things buried in the ground. She speaks Arabic as well as I do, and—"

"*She?*" interrupted Khalil, astonished. "This Shari is a *female?*"

"Hah! What a female!" commented Leo wryly. "Do not make her angry, or she will go bang like a gun."

They stared at him, bemused at the very idea. Moshe stepped rather heavily on Leo's toe and proceeded to explain. "You will find our customs strange," he explained. "Do not take offense that we think of women as equal to men." (Leo snorted in a way that suggested he might not be altogether convinced of this, and Khalil's liking for the tall Yahudi increased.) "And we," Moshe went on firmly, "will not take offense that you consider women inferior. Thus each will be tolerant of the other, and friendship will not be marred with misunderstanding."

This was a new aspect of things. They set it aside for future consideration as the long and polite farewells were concluded. Then the Jewish boys considerately waited until the goats were well up on the hill again before starting the noisy engine. Even so, the dogs had a little trouble keeping the black goat in order as the machine vanished in clouds of acrid yellow-gray dust. And the dogs had to manage alone, for their masters were unaccountably engrossed in staring after the monster with an interest almost amounting to longing.

"I *do* like machines!" discovered Khalil wistfully.

10. REBELLION

The moment Zubaida had been dreading happened on the evening Moussa announced that he was arranging Jasmin's betrothal to Ismail. Jasmin's olive face paled and then flushed, and the sleeping fire behind her eyes erupted.

"I won't!" she shouted, stamping her foot. "He is old and dull and stupid, and he spills food on his dirty beard! I won't marry him! I won't marry anyone! I shall be so wicked no one will have me! I'll go outside and scream, and tell him he is the son of dogs and pigs! I'll cut off all my hair and eyelashes so that I'm ugly! I'll refuse to do any work; I'll refuse to eat; I'll kill myself!"

She stopped, having run out of breath and words alike, and stood panting and glaring into the stupefied silence. The family was frozen, and no one was more astonished than Jasmin herself.

"Bismallah!" exclaimed Moussa at last, unable to take it in.

This unfroze Kbeer Abou's tongue, never long at a

loss. "Scorpion! Bedouine! Shaitan himself has entered her, with many other devils! Have I not always said so? A female twin is twice cursed. Did I not tell thee to bury her at birth? And now she turns on her father, like a wicked unnatural demon! Did I not tell thee to beat her more often? Did I not—"

"Enough!" interrupted Moussa, his own outrage lessened by Kbeer Abou's outburst. The sight of Jasmin's frightened, desolate defiance, like a small animal at bay, softened him further. The child must be half maddened to go to pieces that way! She simply was not herself. He mastered his anger, and spoke with a gentleness no Arab girl could possibly expect after such behavior.

"My daughter, what is the meaning of such talk? Has a devil indeed possessed thee? I have arranged this betrothal for thy happiness, and the marriage will not be yet: not for two years or more. Is Ismail so revolting to thee, then? Hassoun would gladly have thee; he has said so. I did not think he would be as kind as Ismail. Would—" He paused, quite aware that he was breaking custom, but—because he loved her so much—breaking it anyway. He offered her a choice. "Would you rather marry Hassoun?"

It didn't take Khalil's gasp, Mother's and Hayat's startled faces, Kbeer Abou's shock to tell Jasmin what a great concession Father was making. She knew it quite well. But the demon, once released, refused to subside.

"No!" she screeched. "I hate Hassoun even worse! I don't want to marry anyone! I don't," she wailed despairingly, "want to do anything!"

Moussa regarded her with increased severity. "Thou art being unreasonable, my daughter," he pointed out with heroic restraint.

Jasmin deflated. She could have maintained her defiance longer in the face of fury and threats; kindness defeated her. She stood, a forlorn small figure in the center of the room, alone against the world. Her lips drooped. She made one last defense.

"Of course I'm unreasonable," she sniffed. "I'm a female, and nobody expects a female to be reasonable. Nobody," she discovered with fresh grief, "even *lets a* female be reasonable! I might as well be just as unreasonable as I can!"

"A female," her father pointed out with stern sorrow, "is also expected to be humble and obedient. I fear that Kbeer Abou is right, and that I have been too lenient with thee. It is my duty, daughter, to beat thee for sins of insolence and disobedience."

And being a man of duty, he did so. No one enjoyed it. Hayat sobbed aloud, and Zubaida wept silently. Jasmin, with tight-lipped stubbornness worthy of her father, did neither. Khalil found himself unexpectedly sympathetic toward his twin, even wishing that she had been a boy, for she would have made a good one. Even Kbeer Abou, for all his abusive talk, humphed and grumped and said no more. Ahmed watched in bewil-

dered sorrow, and Yusif kept carefully out of sight just
in case someone should get in the spirit of the thing
and remember his own latest misdeeds.

"Now go to bed and pray for a meek and womanly
heart," ordered Moussa when the disagreeable business
was over.

Jasmin, walking stiffly but with head high, moved
silently to the door leading to the outside stairs. She
paused and looked back at Moussa. "I am sorry I was
impudent, oh my father," she murmured. But she did
not say she would marry Ismail; and the lowering of
her heavy brows and the angle of her chin suggested
strongly that the subject was not altogether settled.

There was a tense peace in the house of the mukhtar
the next morning. It was the kind of peace that exists
after an exploratory skirmish, with both forces waiting
to see whether there will be a full-scale battle or not.
Moussa was down from the roof almost as early as the
women, sitting cross-legged on his mat munching figs
and pita, and eyeing his daughter with distress,
thoughtfulness, and new respect. Hah! She had fire and
steel in her, that one! He had not dreamed how much.
It was a pity, in a way. The fire should have gone to
Ahmed, and the steel to Yusif, who seemed to have
none at all. She had pride, too, for although it was clear
from her movements that her back was painful from
the beating, no sign of it touched the calm face she
bent over the long daily task of grinding flour.

But she was quiet again this morning. The astonishing storm of last night had burned out, and there would be no more trouble. He was sorry he had had to beat her.

Jasmin, after one dubious glance from under her lashes, kept her gaze fixed on her work. She was exhausted in mind and body from the burst of passion, the beating, and the long hours of wakefulness afterwards. She wasn't ready for another encounter—yet. But it would come. She wasn't going to marry Ismail, nor Hassoun either. She wondered what would happen to her. Although in theory a girl could refuse the husband her father chose, the thing simply never happened, so there was no precedent . . . Or was there? Was it possible that females *had* defied males before, and that men never mentioned it for fear that other women might get the idea?

It was an encouraging thought. Either it had never happened before, in which case Jasmin was at least remarkable, or it *had* happened before, in which case she was not alone. Her lips set more firmly, and her aching shoulders straightened a little. She dreaded the next clash—but at the same time there was a new thing in her which looked forward to it, like a young warrior who has had his first taste of battle and begins to suspect that he may yet grow to like it.

Kbeer Abou and the boys began to wander in, to grab handsful of whatever suited their fancy before going on with the affairs of the day.

Males, Jasmin decided resentfully, were lazy and

selfish. Father would spend the day walking or talking, or drinking coffee or playing chess, as he wished. Kbeer Abou would drink coffee, gossip, sleep, and work himself up into rages which he enjoyed tremendously. It was true that boys worked until they got married, but it was easier than women's work—especially for Khalil, who led the extremely relaxed life of a goatherd, with Buazza to do most of the work. As for Yusif, privileged to go to school . . .

By the time they were all gone, Jasmin was wearing a distinctly surly expression. Zubaida eyed her daughter anxiously, her thoughts not with the dough she was mixing. Moussa thought the girl had given in, but he was wrong. The flame in Jasmin had by no means gone out; it was just smouldering before breaking forth anew. It brooded in her face as she leaned forward to poke twigs in the fire which had been built in a large earthen pot. Probably she would never be content with woman's role so long as that flame burnt . . . and yet to quench it would make of her a broken creature like Sarika.

Was there no answer, then; no chance of happiness for her daughter? Zubaida closed her eyes and appealed to Allah, even though she had already done so at sunrise prayers.

Jasmin, having tested the sides of the fire-jar for heat, took a ball of the stiff dough and began deftly shaping and flattening it, tossing it back and forth over her forearms until it was paper-thin. Then she spread it against the hot side of the jar, sat back on her heels, and shot out a sullen lower lip.

"It isn't fair!" she announced. "Why should women have to work all the time, and men do hardly anything?"

Zubaida didn't answer. Jasmin knew perfectly well the relative roles of male and female, and what The Prophet had said on the subject. There was no need to go over it again.

Jasmin, having discovered and aired one buried grievance, fished around for another. It wasn't hard to find. "And why should men always ride on the donkeys while women walk and carry all the heavy bundles as well?" she demanded. "Allah made men bigger and stronger, so why does He not mean them to do the harder work?"

"Ipe, Jasmin," said her mother warningly. This was dangerously near heresy.

Jasmin subsided, scowling, to brood over more iniquities. Zubaida discovered the bread burning and hastily tore the flat, curved, smoking sheet off the side of the jar. "Your father must not see this waste!" she fretted. "We will have to eat it ourselves at mid-day."

"Why?" muttered Jasmin mutinously, and Zubaida sighed. Her patience was wearing thin, for all her sympathy, and she had had very little sleep last night, either.

"There is a very big devil in you today," she said. "I think you had better leave the rest of the pita to me and go out for fuel. Perhaps you can leave the devil somewhere before you come back."

Jasmin rose willingly. Action was painful today, but fuel-gathering was her only snatch of freedom, and she grasped at it eagerly. "Yes, Mother," she murmured, sorry to have taken it out on poor Mother, also cursed by having been born a female.

Once outside, she turned eastward without even thinking about it. Kfar Shalom drew her as a magnet. Whatever was it *like* to be a Yahuda? Jasmin's imagination simply shook its head at the suggestion, swearing it didn't know where to begin.

The devil didn't leave her as she glided across the threshing floor and down the other side of the ridge, well out of sight of the village. It rode her shoulders, making her feel wicked and defiant. Her kaftan suddenly became too long and troublesome, and she thought again about the Yahud girls in shorts, working and laughing side by side with men. How could it be? She lurked in a convenient pine grove and stared.

There were the Yahud, quite close, working and talking companionably. A smiling young man took a huge bucket from a tawny-haired girl, seeming to reprove her for lifting something too heavy, and actually carried it himself into the biggest building. Just behind, there were some Yahud on a new shed, finishing the roof. A girl threw something at a man, who caught it, laughed, and tossed it back. The girl ducked neatly, and they all went back to work. Bismallah! They were *playing!* There were concepts here Jasmin simply couldn't begin to grasp. Fascinated, she drew still closer, and the devil whispered in her ear, and rebellion rose again.

Why not? She had already defied her father, and intended to go right on doing so. Having set her hand to that much wickedness, why boggle at a little more? Heart pounding, she walked up to a carob tree that stood close to the biggest building, and stared from behind it, prepared to retreat hastily if anyone should see her.

Another girl came out, heading toward Jasmin, who made herself as small as possible—but stayed there. She might never again get such a good look. Besides, the girl didn't look dangerous. Slim, shapely legs rose in long nakedness to far above the knee, where blue denim shorts began. Somehow they seemed slightly less shocking, either because Jasmin was getting hardened to it or because black skin somehow looks less undressed than light skin. The dark arms, too, were bare, and a white cotton shirt was open at the slender throat. Black hair, cropped short, tossed in ringlets over a shapely head, and the girl had an air of happy unselfconsciousness that was nothing short of astounding.

"Allah!" breathed Jasmin incredulously.

The girl saw her and stopped, peering to see what it was in back of the tree. Jasmin turned to run.

"Salaam!" called the girl. "Wait, oh my sister! Do not run away! Let me greet thee in peace and friendship." She spoke fluent, but oddly accented Arabic.

Jasmin paused. The girl was coming toward her, smiling and beckoning. "Do you live in Bab-il-Howa? Will you do me the honor of visiting a little? Will you come see our village?"

This last was too much even for Jasmin's devil. She shook her head mutely—but her eyes were filled with longing.

"Then let us speak here," suggested the girl, and sat down in the shade of the tree. "Welcome," she smiled. "My name is Chava. What is yours?"

"Jasmin," said Jasmin, unable to tear her fascinated eyes from all that expanse of leg. There was a short silence, and then she looked up to find dark eyes twinkling at her.

"I know just how you feel," confided Chava. "I grew up in an Arab land, dressing like you but with much heavier veils, and when I first came to Palestine I was shocked to death. I wouldn't wear shorts for a long time. So you see, I know just how we look to you. And," she added in sudden mischief, "especially to your men, who say we are altogether indecent and ought to be struck down by bolts of lightning."

Jasmin giggled unexpectedly. It sounded exactly like Kbeer Abou! She felt a sudden bond of affection for Chava, mixed with something she did not yet recognize as envy. "That is so," she agreed. "You should hear my brother! . . . But what of your men? Are they not shocked? Don't they mind? Is it truly all right with them? Aren't you afraid Allah will punish you later on?"

Chava shook her head. "I was at first. We Yahud used to believe as you do about women, you know. Some still do. But now most of us think it was a mistake, and God never intended females to be inferior, but that was something that some men invented and kept going because it was convenient to them . . . Oh dear, I hope I haven't offended you!" she added, troubled.

Jasmin shook her head, enthralled. Chava couldn't have chosen a better psychological moment if she had set out to indoctrinate her. "It's just a complete difference in the way we think about the world and everything," the Jewish girl explained pacifically, watching with understanding as Jasmin's transparent face revealed the whole of her struggle. She was like a young fish trying to comprehend the notion of living in air.

"After all," Chava went on helpfully, "you Arabs have different customs even among yourselves. The Bedouin Arabs undoubtedly consider *you* indecent because their women are much more heavily veiled, and kept much more in *purdah*."

"Oh," said Jasmin, quickly grasping the parallel and tucking it away in her mind to digest later. It might take a good deal of chewing first—but the results might be highly interesting. She smiled.

Chava smiled back, producing a small unexpected pair of dimples in her dark cheeks. "How did you happen to come today?" she asked. "I'll bet you slipped away without permission! Will your people begin to visit us soon, do you think? We do want to be friends, you know."

But Jasmin's face had clouded. "I am being very wicked," she confided. "I'm supposed to be gathering fuel, but I came here to watch. And that," she added with morbid relish, "is the least of my wickedness. Father picked a husband for me and I have refused him, and Father's second choice, as well. What happens," she asked desolately, "if a Yahuda refuses to marry her father's choices?"

Chava was staring, the mahogany-brown of her face puckered in concern. "But surely you are too young, even—" She stopped.

Jasmin sighed. "Oh yes, and Father would not have the marriage until I am fourteen at least. But the betrothal would be now, and," she pointed out with the wisdom of a grandmother, "two years can be a very short time, I think. Are you married? Did you feel happy when you learned who the man was to be?" For Chava looked as if she found life delightful, if one didn't count her distressed expression just now.

"I'm not married," she said gently. "We— Our fathers don't select our husbands for us, Jasmin. We choose each other, man and woman. We come to know and love each other first, before betrothal. Only a few of us here at Kfar Shalom are married, but others will be soon. I have chosen my husband," she confided mischievously, "but Yaacov does not know it yet, and I am being very tactful and giving him some time to find out for himself. But none can be married before seventeen, you see, because the new law—"

But Jasmin had stopped listening. Her eyes perfect circles, she was contemplating this heaven-upon-earth incredulously.

"I—I wish I were a Yahuda!" she blurted. "May Allah forgive me," she added with a pacifying glance at the burning blue of the sky.

Chava was thinking intently. "Perhaps Allah will aid you in some way," she suggested tentatively. Jasmin shook her head, quite definite about that. Allah aid a rebellious and undutiful female? Never!

In the face of her misery, Chava threw discretion to the desert. "Well, whether Allah does or not," she declared, "Israel will. That's the new government," she explained to the bewildered small face, which was not yet daring to hope. "There are new laws being passed. One is that there must be only one wife to one husband in future, and another is that people cannot marry until they are at least seventeen. Your father doesn't know this yet, I'm sure, but he'll know it long before two years are up."

Jasmin considered this doubtfully. For one thing, she didn't think Father would for a moment permit some Israeli law to interfere with his affairs. And for another, a postponement of the marriage didn't really help the immediate problem of the betrothal. She pointed this out somberly.

Chava saw the problem at once. She frowned. "I'll

talk to Avram," she promised. "Are you truly determined, Jasmin? Can you hold out for a little longer? Be
tactful, or ill, or anything to delay the betrothal for a
while. I'm sure we can help. Just have courage. And of
course don't tell *anyone* you've spoken to any of us."

Jasmin didn't need to be warned of that! Not even
Mother was safe. She glanced nervously up to where
the flat roofs of a few village houses could just be seen
over the ridge, and wriggled further under the tree,
just in case. Thank goodness there was a wadi, with a
struggling line of Jerusalem pines and scrub oaks, that
gave her cover to a spot where the ridge itself quite hid
her from Bab-il-Howa.

"I'd better go now," she said uneasily, but didn't
move for a moment. If only—

The slim black hand squeezed her slender brown
one. "Can you come again without being caught?"
asked Chava. "Do try! As often as you can do it safely!
Next time you'll come see our kibbutz, won't you? And
meet the other girls, and make friends. And remember,
we will help you, I promise; trust us."

"Thank you!" stammered Jasmin. "Allah bless you!
I—" She sped away, eyes shining with tears and new
ideas, and with the devil on her shoulder suddenly less
sulky but a great deal less submissive, as well. There
was a certain new look in the set of her chin when she
finally arrived home which caused fresh concern to
Zubaida—who was not one bit reassured at her daughter's sudden and suspicious air of saintliness.

At Kfar Shalom, Chava had a talk with Avram, who at once made a report to the new Government Department of Arab Affairs. Things were set in motion. In all the confusion and complexity of organizing a brand new nation in the midst of enemies, the troubles of one small female were not overlooked.

"After all," said a tired minister, "if we lose sight of individual people, we might as well not have bothered." And taking out a map, he began to mark villages in Achula Valley.

11. the law

Summer crept along, and the grapes were ripening under Ahmed's solicitous eyes when a battered car stopped at the bottom of the village and a black-mustached Arab with voluminous robes and a green turban paced slowly and with dignity up the road. He was escorted to the mukhtar's house by Mahmoud, whose bright old eyes sparkled with curiosity and interest—and also reverence. That green turban meant that its wearer had made the holy pilgrimage to Mecca.

Moussa regarded them with resignation. What now? There had been too many strangers coming here lately; it unsettled his people and his children. Where were the old secure days when the world had obligingly let them alone? But Moussa knew what hospitality demanded, and he invited Mahmoud and the stranger in with grave courtesy.

Jasmin might easily have missed the visit had she been allowed to go for fuel as she had wished. But Zubaida, suspicious, had put her foot down and sent

Hayat, causing Jasmin to darken like a thundercloud.
Now the sun broke out, and she fairly wriggled inside
the loose kaftan.

"Ipe!" said her mother warningly. One of these days
Moussa was going to notice that his daughter took an
entirely disproportionate interest in his business conversations. Moreover, the girl was far too cheerful and
downright sanctimonious lately—neither trait at all in
character under the circumstances. Zubaida gave her a
quelling frown as she placed a platter of ripe fruit into
the small hands. But Jasmin merely put on an air of
outrageous meekness as she served Moussa and his
guests.

When the fruit, and then tiny cups of thick, sweet
coffee had been finished, there was polite silence for a
few moments. No need to rush headlong into business.
Westerners might, but then they have no notion of lei-
sure or subtlety or the proper use of time. The courteous ritual followed in a sonorous flow that would
have delighted the soul of Alouf.

At last the guest, who had introduced himself as
Qassab al-Sayid, looked at his host with a peculiarly
sweet smile. Jasmin watched his profile, enchanted.
What a remarkable nose! A beak of a nose! A magnificent nose, curving downward from the high forehead
in one continuous arc. One couldn't really say that his
face had a nose, but almost that the nose wore a face!

"I come," said Qassab, "from the Israeli Department
of Arab Affairs."

Father's eyebrows bunched. "How is this? Thou art an Arab, surely?"

"I am an Arab." The nose nodded tranquilly. "I am also an Israeli."

"Hah!" The eyebrows scrambled themselves. "A Yahudi?"

"No, an Arab; I told thee so. But an Israeli because I live in the nation of Israel. Thou, too, oh Mukhtar, are an Israeli."

This was a matter of such astonishment to Jasmin that her mother had to pinch her to hold her still. Fortunately, Moussa was also too startled to notice the bouncing in the women's corner. He pondered it, finding it a thing he had not thought of before.

"No one asked me," he pointed out reprovingly. "It was not my choice."

"Nor mine," agreed Qassab. "But then, rare is the man who can choose his nationality. Most are born to it."

Mahmoud stirred and spoke, his voice high and sweet considering the volume it had when he called prayers five times daily. "Such things are Allah's choice," he said. "Thanks be to Him that we were born Arabs."

"*Il hamdillah!*" echoed Qassab. "I thank God, also, that I have now become an Israeli. I am grateful for both blessings, and would not choose to leave Israel."

Moussa was clearly smelling rats. "I would not choose to leave my village," he conceded with a caution that made his daughter grin knowingly. "But why should I be glad that the Yahud have taken this land? They are not my people, nor their ways my ways."

"Nevertheless, we are now one nation. In some matters our peoples will go their separate ways; in others we must now take the same way. That is as it should be."

His disarming manner didn't in the least disguise the smell of interference. Moussa maintained a granite silence. It was the imam who asked in what things the road must be the same.

"In national laws, to begin with," said Qassab. "All nations have them, you know. There will be some changes now from the old Turkish or English ones."

Moussa chose to pretend he'd never heard of this. He pursed his lips judiciously. "I am Mukhtar of Bab-il-Howa. It is I who say what my people will do."

Qassab, who should have been struck into silence, merely sucked tranquilly at the water pipe which Moussa had provided. "You have a son, perhaps, who is a goatherd?"

It was a safe guess. Most Arab families did. Moussa nodded warily.

"Your son tells the goats and sheep what to do, and they obey him?"

Jasmin began to see the drift of this. So, doubtless, did her father, for he frowned. Jasmin bounced again with excitement, and again her mother administered a sharp poke. Qassab went on, implacably.

"However, thy son in turn obeys thee. He does not tell the goats to do things which you forbid. In Israel you are the goatherd but the Law is the mukhtar."

"My son knows me," Moussa objected. "I do not know the Law."

"I am here to tell you of it; then you will know."

Moussa jutted his beard forward and looked ominous. "Tell me, then."

Qassab felt like a man trying to tame an enraged bull on the edge of a precipice. At best Moslem Arabs disliked laws which went against their religious custom, and Israel was trying to be very slow and gentle about such changes. Moussa, like many, threatened to be extremely prickly and stubborn, and Qassab decided to mention the law most pertinent just now. But there was no use trying to sidle up to it. He decided to be blunt.

"There is to be henceforth a law regarding child marriages," he said, and was careful not to notice the sudden agitation in the corner. "No one may marry under the age of seventeen." And he braced himself for the explosion.

It was surprisingly halfhearted. Moussa muttered and grumbled as a matter of principle, but he found himself rather relieved. It was a splendid excuse for postponing a marriage which he had begun to think not a very good idea, after all. Jasmin was surely a girl out of the ordinary, far more intelligent and spirited and courageous than most females. He had been wondering whether she might not be wasted on Ismail, worthy of someone far more important. Better to break the betrothal negotiations altogether; an easy enough thing, since he had not yet accepted the bride-price . . .

"Yahud interference!" he growled with remarkably little passion. "Next they will try to tell us how many wives we can have!"

As a matter of fact, they would, but Qassab judged that this was not the best time to mention it. "There is also a matter of schools," he went on. "We will provide them for every village as rapidly as we can, and presently it will be the law that all children attend."

Moussa had been about to inform him proudly that Bab-il-Howa already had a school, but this last bit struck the thought from his mind. "*All* children?" he echoed, not knowing that his daughter was ahead of him; that she was already gripping her mother's hand with sudden fierce hope. "Surely you mean all *male* children."

Qassab shook his green turban. "*All* children," he repeated.

"Then it is a very bad law," pronounced Moussa, profoundly disapproving. "It is against Allah's will that females be educated; moreover it is unnatural, and too great a strain on them. Besides, what man would want a wife who knows as much as he? Also," he pointed out darkly, "it's liable to give women ideas. They'll end up thinking themselves the equal of men."

Jasmin made a muffled noise against Zubaida's

shoulder. They already did, some of them! And Jasmin, having by now made several more visits to Kfar Shalom, was beginning to absorb the shattering notion herself. Her heresy had not yet progressed so far as to make her seriously question her father's omniscience—but the first step had been taken. She sat now, breathless with the possibility of education that Qassab had suddenly dangled before her.

Moussa was regarding his guest dubiously. "You speak like a very great heretic," he told him, a stern eye on the green turban.

The magnificent nose did not so much as flare a nostril. "Nay," said its owner with calm. "Where in the Koran does it say that females may not be educated?"

Moussa turned to Mahmoud, but the old man just shook his head, clearly enjoying himself greatly.

"Is it possible," Qassab went on, "that thou, oh Moussa, art inadvertently committing sacrilege thyself? Who has the right to dictate to Allah? Tell me if I am wrong, oh Imam. If a thing happens, it is Allah's will. Many hundreds of years ago He sent His Prophet to tell the Faithful His rules for them. Now the world changes—also by Allah's will, since no other thing can happen—and it may be that some of these old rules are no longer suitable. Will you—" and he turned almost accusingly to Moussa—"Will you forbid Allah the right to permit change? Will you say to him, 'Because a thing has been so it must always be so, for I, Man, say so'?"

No one answered this. Jasmin, panting almost audibly, took back every disrespectful thought she had ever held about Allah. Oh, please, please: just a breath, a taste, a touch of education!

Qassab seemed to be working toward that very end. Surely he was an angel, straight from Michael! "Many of us have noticed in recent years that Allah has been creating females of great spirit and intelligence here and there. Is this an accident? Does Allah make mistakes? Or does He intend that His gifts should be nourished and developed wherever they happen, to be used to His greater glory?"

Mahmoud nodded vigorously. Moussa shot him a reproachful glance and sat in silence for a few moments. On one hand, the man might almost be describing Jasmin. On the other, this was a novel idea, and therefore dangerous. Moreover, Moussa had the feeling he was being, somehow, double-talked.

"I do not admit all this," he said at last. "But even if it is true what has that to do with ordinary females? Let the Law, if it wishes, find and train these girls who are gifted of Allah. But that is no reason to ruin all the rest by educating them."

"Then thy village has no gifted ones?" Qassab looked surprised. "I should have expected the daughters of a man such as thee—" He paused, apparently trying to be tactful, yet clearly astonished that Moussa had not passed on his qualities of mind.

Moussa stirred uncomfortably on his cushions. Jas-

min was indeed such a one—but it would be very bad
to encourage this. What good would education do her?
Stir her up, make her the more restless when she had
just got over that recent extraordinary spell, ruin her
chance of getting a good husband. No! He shook his
head stubbornly. In the corner Jasmin, having
glimpsed Paradise, now saw it recede.

"It is better for girls to learn womanly things," her
father was explaining kindly. "It prepares them for
their proper role in life. As to boys, Mahmoud already
has a school for them where he teaches the Koran and
some reading, and many stay in it for as long as three
or four years."

Mahmoud stirred. "I am an old man. Every year little boys become harder to teach. I think perhaps I
should like the Law to take this task from my shoulders. Does it send teachers?"

"Yahud teachers?" interposed Moussa suspiciously.
"Unbelievers?"

The nose pointed itself at him. "Certainly not," said
Qassab. "We are trying very hard to find and train
enough Arab teachers, though there are far too few,
since few Arabs have sent their sons to school to learn.
We do our best, but—" He paused, then sent his
shrewdest arrow. "It may be some time before there
will be one available to thee, since so many villages are
very eager that their children not remain ignorant."

Moussa reacted just as he was intended to. Pride in
his village rose. Were others to have advantages denied

his people? Would other men's sons lord it over his some day? His beard thrust forward. "If the Law says there shall be schools, then the Law must provide them to all. I demand my rights as an Israeli! I shall complain to this Knesset! Surely the law must also obey itself?"

Qassab nodded admiringly. "That is truly spoken. The Law will be very careful not to demand school attendance before it can supply the schools. Still, the teachers now available must be put to best use, and there are ten, twenty, places for each. And if you were the Law, oh Mukhtar, and had one teacher to place, would you put him in an area where all children will be sent until the age of twelve, or where only some of the children will come for a few years?" He paused to let this sink in, and then gave his host a cheerful smile. "Never mind. Children from thy neighboring villages will doubtless study to become teachers, and they some day can come and teach thy grandchildren."

Moussa breathed heavily. Pride and stubbornness battled. "I must think about it," he announced, suddenly relieved. Thinking about it would be a long process. No need to decide now. "You may tell the Law," he told Qassab, still not hauling down his banner, "that they may begin looking for a *good* teacher for my village. If he is good enough, it is possible that I may permit very young females to attend for a while."

It was a shattering concession. Everyone in the room realized it. Qassab, wise enough not to press his luck, bowed the green turban with an air of reverence. "Thou art wise indeed, oh Mukhtar. I shall tell the Law thy words, and also that thou art a diamond of a man, whose children may also prove to be diamonds. Israel will need such to be her leaders in future years," he added thoughtfully, rising. "But that is in the hands of Allah. A thousand thanks for thy hospitality, oh Mukhtar, and for the honor of conversation with thee."

"The honor is mine," returned Moussa, escorting his guest out through the blue door and into the street.

But in the corner Jasmin, hope snatched away a second time, since she was already twelve, sobbed bitterly and wrenchingly. She hated Allah!

12. REVENGE

Ahmed stood on the edge of village fields staring over at the kibbutz land. So many strange things! The big machines that plowed swift and deep, so very much deeper than the scratches of a wooden plow; the bringing of water where water did not flow naturally; the crops and seedling trees altogether foreign to Ahmed, tended by the yellow-haired boy who might almost be Ahmed's twin under the skin, and who was certainly his friend. Not that they had exchanged words other than an occasional shy greeting, of course, but that was not important. Some day, no doubt, they would get around to talking, provided the Yahudi could speak enough Arabic to make it possible. When that happened, Ahmed was collecting a number of questions he wanted to ask. In the meantime they just watched each other and were friends. There was no hurry.

Selim, diffidently approaching the foot of Kfar Shalom, felt altogether differently about this last point. There *was* a hurry. He wanted to learn so many things, and he was getting very old, being already thirteen, and soon it would be too late. What good to have been Mahmoud's prize pupil, probably the best reader in the village, when there was nothing to read? Soon he would forget.

But here at least were new people with new viewpoints on things, from whom he could learn much. Moreover, they had books. Selim had seen a box of them being carried in one day. Now he found himself hovering near the main building as Jasmin had done before him, telling himself firmly that the books would be in Hebrew, anyway, and he had no business being here.

But before he could cause himself to vanish again, Leo came around a corner arguing loudly with a girl who might have been Arabic but for her clothing . . . or, rather, lack of it. Selim averted his eyes, embarrassed. Leo saw him, instantly forgot the argument, and shouted a welcome.

"Shalom, shalom! I mean, salaam! About time you came to see us!" His Arabic was comically mixed with Hebrew, but intelligible. "This is Shari, remember? The girl who goes bang. I told you about her. Shari, this is Selim."

Selim regarded Shari with interest. It was true, she did go bang at Leo in a way, sputtering an indignant mixture of Hebrew and Arabic. But it was clear that the Arabic was for Selim's benefit, and that both of them really quite enjoyed going bang at each other. He saw, too, that there was no evil in Shari, despite her indecorous dress and behavior. Perhaps he would even get used to this presently. Somehow, he kept thinking of Jasmin every time one of these long-limbed, independent girls went past.

Before he knew it, he was feeling very much at home, helping Leo with his chores, meeting half a dozen Yahud of both sexes. He was a little surprised at how comfortable he felt, although it was not really astonishing. Selim's nature was to like people, ignoring superficials like appearance or custom, and going right to the inside person. By the time the afternoon had sped, he had picked up a dozen words of Hebrew, and a girl named Malkah had promised to send for some books in Arabic for him.

Not that there was much sitting around being sociable. Yahud hospitality appeared to consist of making a guest one of themselves, talking as they worked. And how they worked, men and women alike, pushing themselves as if all eternity were not time enough to do everything! Planting, watering, fertilizing, tending animals, building furniture and sheds. A baking house was in use now, and a carpenter shop and machine shop, and a place where dirty clothes were put in *hot* water with a powder that made white bubbles! Someone had even found time to set up a rough bench under the wide shade of a butterfly tree, and plant a bit of grass, a few seedling trees, a handful of flowers!

"That would be Judy," explained Shari kindly, making sure a tawny-haired Yahuda heard her. "She can't help it; she came from a place called England where they all have a madness for growing flowers, even if it takes what little spare time they have."

The tawny-haired girl—presumably Judy—laughed and made a face at Shari and vanished. Shari, who had appointed herself Selim's guide when Leo went on patrol duty, cast a proud eye over the fledgling village. "You see, we have flat land by the river and also part of the hill," she explained. "We will drain swamp where we need to, and use river water to irrigate, and build our living units and buildings here. On the slopes of the hill we can have orchards, and— Why are you looking like that?"

"But when will you pause to enjoy it all?" Selim demanded, appalled. "You are too energetic! You will race through life and never notice that it is good and beautiful!"

He half expected her to go bang, but she did no such thing. Instead, she gave him a rather sweet smile. "I know what you mean," she confessed. "I came from a place called India, where we knew how to sit and think and dream, too. Perhaps some day we will learn to do it here . . . though I doubt it," she added honestly. "We enjoy working like this, truly we do. We are building something. We have a land of our own for the first time in two thousand years, Selim; did you know that? We have wandered the earth, exiled, alien in all other lands no matter how many centuries we might live there. 'Jew' became a term of insult."

Selim nodded. It still was—though he had not

known this was true everywhere. How enlightening to
have this glimpse through Yahud eyes!

"But now that you have your land," he persisted,
"why do you not sit down and enjoy it?"

Shari looked shocked. "But it isn't ready to enjoy!
There is so much to do! The land is in a terrible state.
The Turks did much of that, I have heard; wherever
they went, they destroyed the land, like goats. We must
bring water where it is needed, and put fertilizer in the
soil, and find new crops to grow, and build industry,
and homes and schools, and teach Hebrew, and bring
in all the Yahud all over the world who wish to come,
and find work and homes for them, and run electricity
and telephones and water and sewage, and build hospi-
tals and clinics, and train teachers and nurses and doc-
tors and social workers and archeologists, and work out
a government. Selim, we want to make it a new kind of
country, better than any before; where people care
about other people, and where even the government
cares more about justice than advantage, and more
about kindness than justice."

Selim's eyes were bulging slightly. They were quite
mad, all of them, of course. They seemed to be trying
to improve upon nature and man: a thing very near
sacrilege. But there was something magnificent about
the madness . . . Something contagious . . . "Teachers,"
he repeated thoughtfully, and Shari cocked her head to
one side at something in his voice. "What does it mean,
to train teachers?"

Shari lit up with enthusiasm. "Of course! You'd make a splendid teacher, Selim! The government would send you to school and teach you all the things you need to know, to teach others. Would your father permit it?"

Selim hesitated. Father, yes. But the mukhtar? He doubted that Moussa would at all approve. There might be great difficulties. Somehow he did not doubt that he could overcome them . . . somehow . . .

Lost in the future, he came around the corner of the woman's dormitory and caught a definite glimpse of a snuff-colored kaftan and slender bare feet and half-veiled ebony hair being whisked inside by a black-skinned Yahuda. He stared at the dark oblong of door, now smugly blank, not sure whether to believe his eyes or not. He looked at Shari and did believe them, for she was looking alarmed, guilty, pleading, and very much ready to go bang.

"She *needs* to come visit us!" she said fiercely. "She's lonely and unhappy, and hungry in her mind; she needs us. Besides, we give her dry dung. You won't tell, will you?" she declared, rather than asked. "It doesn't hurt anything! But her father—"

Her father, indeed! Moussa's rage would be very great, and justly. It was wrong to deceive and disobey. Still, Moussa had never forbidden his villagers to visit Kfar Shalom. This was entirely because it never entered his head that any would dare do so, but—who was Selim to cause trouble, especially to Jasmin? Had

Shari known it, her plea was quite unnecessary. Selim looked at her, his almond-shaped face bland.

"Who?" he asked in surprise. "I have not seen any-one."

It was fully a week later that Khalil got around to doing the thing that had been on his mind ever since the encounter with the sick jeep. Those Yahud boys hadn't been condescending or superior, but merely friendly. And they knew about machines, of which there were many at the kibbutz . . .

Khalil didn't dream that anyone else had beat him to it. Jasmin was very careful indeed to keep her visits secret, and even Selim, for once, had not confided in his best friend. One could not be quite sure how Khalil would react. To be sure, he seemed mollified toward the Yahud since the affair of the sick jeep, but there was also still a thing in his heart that was defensive and prickly and ready to take offense easily. Best not to mention it for a while.

And so, on a hot September afternoon, Khalil sauntered casually over to the kibbutz, head high, smooth face very much a mask of indifference because of the uncertainty in his breast.

But the pleasure in Moshe's face was unmistakably genuine. "Ho, salaam, Khalil!" he shouted. "Come on; you're just in time. I go to work now in the machine shop. Would you like to come help?"

Khalil was very late coming home that night, and his

mother wondered greatly about that black greasy stuff he had got all over his aba and tob and even his new red-and-white striped khaffiya. And for the second time, too!

The olive harvest was upon them, and once again the entire village turned out to get them gathered before the rains. It was a tawny day, a hot day with the peculiar mellow heat of early October, a rich and fun-filled day. The men and older boys beat the olives out of the gnarled trees with long sticks, while the smaller and more agile lads climbed high into the branches to reach the ones in the treetops. Below, women and tiny tots gathered the blackly shining globules from the ground into huge baskets. There was laughter and shouting and singing; and when it was done and the ground bare and yellow, Moussa set aside those baskets which were to be divided and pickled. The others went to the oil press, where they would be crushed by a huge stone wheel into a black pulp which was then put into tough grass baskets.

Khalil enjoyed this part. He liked to see the baskets piled five or six high on the stone slab, and then to watch the huge beam forced down and down until the olive oil flowed from the sides of the baskets, along the gutters of the stone slab, and into the stone trough, from where it was drawn off into goatskins and jars. The whole process appealed to him. It was ingenious and efficient and interesting. And when it occurred to him to wonder whether the Yahud had invented a way even better and more efficient, he pushed the thought away angrily.

There were a few vague clouds in the west that evening, a sure sign of coming rain, at this season. The next day was spent cleaning out the cisterns and the water-channels leading to them. Then there was time to take the goats out once more before the rains. Clouds were just beginning to gather; there was still a day or two.

Alouf went up the hill, Selim along the westward slopes, and Khalil took his herd down into the valley, past the spot where he and Selim had met the jeep, where there was still enough grass for a little grazing. He sat under a scrub oak not far from the road, and contemplated. Next season Yusif ought to take over the work of goatherd. Khalil was getting too old for it, and bored as well. He wanted to— to—

To what? Khalil didn't know. He sighed, his life a vast restless confusion. He wanted to do things with machines! He discovered it suddenly, and with a sense of dismay. For it was perfectly certain that Father would never consider such a thing.

Deep in his brooding, he didn't hear the approaching jeep until it clattered and roared around the bend of the road, sending half a dozen of the nearest goats in headlong flight up the hill. Khalil jumped to his feet to help Buazza head them off, saw that the dog was doing very well by himself, and contented himself with the

little chirping call "Easy, easy; it is all right; be calm."
Then, the crisis over, he saw that the jeep had stopped.

A lean head poked itself out of the window, and
Khalil saw, with a throb of particularly active dislike,
that it belonged to Major Schorr.

"You! Boy!" called the major in a commanding tone
that set Khalil's teeth on edge. "Come here!"

Khalil did not move a muscle, except to curl his lip
slightly. He remained standing, a slim, proud figure,
the very folds of his aba motionless.

"Did you hear me?" shouted Major Schorr. "I said,
come here! I want to talk to you."

Khalil deliberately sat down. His mind felt cool and
clear, as it never did when he argued with Jasmin, and
he had a sense of sureness and of time.

"I do not wish to come there," he said in a dispas-
sionate voice that he knew instinctively would infuri-
ate this Yahudi as nothing else. "Nor do I desire to talk
with you." And pulling out his little flute he played a
few elaborately mocking notes.

The officer reddened, muttered something in Hebrew, and Khalil needed no translation for the general
meaning. It began to dawn on him with bright clarity
that he had the upper hand. Major Shorr had made the
tactical error of making a demand which he could not
enforce. What would he do next? Khalil considered the
possibilities. To give up and drive off would be to lose
face; to come and speak to Khalil under the tree would
would be worse. If he sent his driver to fetch Khalil,

Khalil could simply retreat up the hill, or even set
Buazza on them. There was always the gun in the officer's holster . . . For a moment Khalil's heart twisted,
and he gave a swift glance at the tree trunk, which
would not be very much protection. But he did not
move.

The major was muttering to his driver. Now he
shouted again at the boy. "Little fool; I am not going
to hurt you," he said, although it must have been quite
evident that Khalil was not suffering from timidity.
"Come here, I say! I have something to tell you."

Khalil decided that the man would not shoot him. It
would make too much trouble. A bubbling sense of
triumph began to rise to his head. He played a few
more flute notes, every gesture and sound barbed with
that searing impudence in which the Arab excels.
Then he paused to give the fuming officer a long, contemptuous look.

"I have no wish to hear it," he said, and turned his
head away.

"You had better hear it!" Major Schorr was by now
in a blistering rage. "I recognize you; you are from
Bab-il-Howa, and you are not giving me a very good
impression of your village, let me warn you. I had
intended to speak kindly to you," he added bitterly,
and Khalil fumed at the overtones of patronage in his
voice. "I should have known better. You Arabs are all
the same: you're filthy, whining, sneaky, two-faced,
cowardly, blood-thirsty savages. You'll always stab us in

the back, however often we forgive you, however much we do for you; we're fools to let you stay in Israel at all. Drive on, Eli."

He withdrew his head and the jeep drove on, leaving Khalil the victor—but quivering with white rage. Gone was confusion and indecision; Khalil knew only one thing. Revenge. Such insults could be wiped out only with blood. He tucked his flute back into his belt, and found that his hands were shaking with the most violent anger he had ever known. This would be paid! By the beard of the Prophet, that Yahudi would pay with his life!

Khalil made a deliberate effort to calm himself, for a cool head was needed. Major Schorr could only be going to Kfar Shalom on this road, and he would probably stay the night there, and leave at dawn for it was getting late. Moreover, Moshe had once said this was his habit on these visits. That gave Khalil the night, then, to plan and act. There would be no more nonsense with magic dynamite that did not go bang; there were at least four or five rifles illegally hidden in the village; Jawad had told him so. Hassoun, Jawad, and Ali would be glad to help. They had taunted him more than once lately, asking if he was now turned Jewlover.

Khalil got to his feet and started home, hardly knowing whether the goats followed or not. He was visualizing the road leading from Kfar Shalom. There was rough ground and thick brush in several places, and several dry wadis: plenty of cover for several ambushers with their rifles. And it would be a dark night, with thickening clouds covering the moon ... If only Allah would cause the major to drive away before the sun was up! Then no one would see, no one be able to prove anything.

It was dusk when Khalil reached Bab-il-Howa and put the goats away. It was dark when the group of four met in Jawad's house, and still later when they reached a decision. For although Khalil had his plan complete, there must always be much argument and discussion and waving of arms before deciding a thing. The night was half over by the time Khalil had gone home to bed, waited for his father's snores, and slipped silently away again.

For a wonder they were all there, three other shadows waiting just below the village. With elaborate precautions they moved downward, blending themselves into the ground on both sides of the road leading from Kfar Shalom. And in the weird gray-black of a storm-threatened dawn, a jeep finally left the kibbutz and rattled along the road toward the valley center.

Four shots rang out, and four shadows scuttled away in triumph.

13. and RETRIBUTION

Moussa awoke suddenly just before dawn with the vague sense that something was wrong. He lay still and thought.

There were things enough to worry him. The outside world was slowly beating down his defenses and penetrating his village, and the result was trouble, as he had always known it would be. The Yahudi-haters shouted less—but they had their heads together more, which was a dangerous sign. No telling when they might do something rash and get caught, bringing the wrath of the Law upon the village. Threats of evacuation had no effect on them; either they did not believe it or they did not care very greatly.

At the other extreme, there were those like Selim and his father who were far too willing to establish casual friendship with Kfar Shalom. Kassem had gone so far as to suggest friendly visiting back and forth, and had even mentioned Selim's desire to be trained as a teacher. Moussa was not at all sure that this was a good idea.

Even in his own family there was trouble. Khalil had been restless and irritable since the Yahud began building their kibbutz, and Moussa felt that something was very wrong with Jasmin lately. Even the post-ponement of her betrothal had failed to produce the gratitude and joy he had expected, but instead a look almost of hunger, as if she hoped for something more —although only Allah knew what it might be! Ah well, she was only a girl-child after all, and at a difficult age as well.

Unable to sleep any more, he arose, and went up to the roof to watch a threatening sunrise . . . and also, as it turned out, to watch Kfar Shalom, which seemed to be in a state of great activity. Too great. There was emergency in the very way they moved, even at this distance. Moussa stared with growing uneasiness. He could not see the abandoned jeep in the road below, nor the four figures by now cowering exultantly but nervously in Jawad's house, but he knew something evil had happened. And when three figures left the kibbutz and walked toward Bab-il-Howa, Moussa got up, left the rooftop, and walked down the hill to meet them.

Avram was in the lead, with two very young men behind, trouble in all three faces, as Moussa had known there would be. He frowned. More dynamite? Or worse? His face was calm and his head high as they met and regarded one another soberly. Avram, search-ing his face, knew that the next hour would probably seal the good will or hostility of this man toward all Israel. Avram had grown up among men like Moussa, understood them, and liked them; liked them far better than he did Major Schorr and his kind. Instinctively he said the right thing.

"Salaam, oh, Mukhtar. I see you have already guessed that grave trouble is upon our villages. I have come to thee for help and advice. Perhaps together we may yet bring good out of evil."

Moussa relaxed imperceptibly. It was better to work with this man, whom he already respected, than against him. Moreover, it was often lonely, standing solitary at the top of his society. It was not unpleasant to have another mukhtar to share problems, even if it was only a young Yahudi who needed the guidance of greater experience.

"We will talk alone," he decided, and led the way back up the hill and through the village to his house.

Selim, coming from his own door, saw them: saw that it was Dan and Leo with Avram, saw the misery in Dan's face and the taut anger on Leo's. Their eyes met, and Selim fell in behind, to stand with his two friends outside the mukhtar's blue door after Moussa and Avram had gone in. Villagers gathered, curious but not seriously alarmed. Yusif and Ahmed came out of the house, Yusif to stare fixedly at Leo, and Ahmed to join his friend Dan in silent companionship. Selim noticed with dismay that Khalil was nowhere to be seen, and his eyes turned to Leo's again, questioning.

Leo nodded brusquely, fists clenched. "You'll hear
soon enough," was all he could say, and they went on
standing while women and children came closer and
the sun vanished beneath the gathering bunches of
cloud.

Inside the house Moussa scrupulously offered coffee,
but took no offense when it was refused. This was no
time to cling to ritual. The world had once more invaded the village and again shattered tradition. In the
corner Jasmin waited hopefully to hear whatever it
was, and found to her great disgust that she could
scarcely catch a word. They spoke in low voices, and it
was apparently of most serious importance.

"Major Schorr," murmured Avram. ". . . provocation . . . jeep . . . understandable . . . keep the army out
of it if we can."

And then Father, his voice low, tense, bitterly angry.
". . . no excuse . . . warned them . . . punishment."

It seemed clear that somehow Father and Avram
were on the same side, which was comforting but puzzling, and they both seemed to be very angry at
"them," but Jasmin couldn't decide whether or not
"them" was that Major Schorr. She nearly perished
from such tantalizing snippets for a full ten minutes
while they talked. Then they went outside, and she
could hear Father give orders for all males over ten to
assemble.

In seconds Jasmin was at her post behind the partly-
open door, hoping passionately that Father wouldn't

decide to move down to the village center for whatever he was going to say . . . No, he wasn't. He was bringing them into the courtyard just outside the door! Jasmin sighed with relief, moved over a gracious few inches to give her mother and Hayat room, and proceeded to concentrate.

"Men of Bab-il-Howa," said Moussa when all were gathered, "listen well. My friend Avram, mukhtar of Kfar Shalom, has brought me bitter news. Before dawn this morning, shots were fired at a jeep which left the kibbutz, and men were seen to run up the road to this village afterwards." He paused. "Either some men from over the border have used my village without my knowledge, or some of ye, my own people, have ignored my commands and committed treachery and violence against our neighbors."

There was a murmur and stir among the men, and Avram took the moment to speak in a low, earnest voice to Moussa, who listened and then raised his robed arm for silence. "My friend Avram, who is more forgiving than he should be, says that there may have been provocation. He says that the Major Schorr, who spoke discourteous words when he came here, visited Kfar Shalom yesterday. He says the major's driver reported that the major was offensive to a boy in the hills, who he said belonged to this village. I say this is no excuse. Ye all heard my words and commands. Some of ye have chosen to disobey and must take the consequences."

He stopped, and his deep-set eyes searched the group of men deliberately. Jasmin, peering out, found her eyes fixed on Khalil, near the edge of the group, with a face like a mask. Her heart gave a lurch. Khalil had done it! She knew as well as if she had seen it happen! For a moment she almost disliked her Yahud friends, who, because they existed, had caused this. Khalil was her twin! However she hated him, it was somehow because she loved him.

"There are faces missing," announced Moussa with irony. "I do not see Jawad, nor Hassoun, nor Ali. I wonder why?" Nervous laughter rippled the crowd. "Some of you go to the house of Jawad and see if they are there," commanded Moussa, "for I think that this concerns them very much indeed." He spared a disparaging glance for the fathers of Hassoun and Ali, and turned a speculative eye upon Kbeer Abou, who at once began sputtering.

"I am innocent!" he squalled, indignant. "Once again they did not let me help! No one ever tells me anything: I, who am oldest and wisest of all!" And he glared at his son-in-law.

Khalil, whose anger had not planned this far ahead, found himself beginning to regret his haste. He had somehow supposed that he could brazen it out, or that nothing would be said in the village at all. Now he perceived that lying would do him no good. For one thing, Father would see through it at once, and for another, his co-conspirators, already under suspicion,

would certainly see to it that Khalil did not escape.
Choosing the least undignified of two evils, he lifted
his chin and stepped forward just as several men appeared with the three suspects in tow.

"It is I who am guilty, Father," he announced defiantly.

An instant later Jawad lifted his own voice. "It was
thy son, oh Mukhtar! It was his doing, and not ours!
We had nothing to do with it. We don't even know a
thing about it! Besides," he added, aggrieved, "that
fool Ali nearly shot me instead of the jeep."

Khalil flashed him one look of bright scorn before
turning to face his father's incredulous wrath.

"Thou! My son!" Moussa's face aged and his eyes
blazed dark lightning. "Thou! Treacherous, perfidi-
ous, disobedient one! Son of Shaitan! Possessed of evil
devils! Why have you brought this disgrace upon my
head? I shall disown thee!"

Everyone stood silent in the grip of this tragic
drama. No one dared move lest the thunderbolt strike
him. Only Avram recklessly laid a hand upon Moussa's
arm. "Since it is I who represent the injured, may I
speak, oh Mukhtar?" he asked.

"This is between my son and me!" Moussa blazed.
Then he turned, paused, calmed himself. "Forgive my
anger. Aye, you have a right to speak."

Avram turned to Khalil, who was still and white beneath the tan of his skin. "Tell me, was it you whom
Major Schorr met on the road yesterday?" Khalil

nodded, speechless. "I thought so," said Avram gently. "Was it a very great insult? So great that you felt that only blood could wash it away?" Again Khalil nodded, surprised that this Yahudi understood. "The major is not an evil man," said Avram sadly. "But he is an un-pleasant one who doubtless causes many of your people to hate my people more than they did before. I can understand thy feelings, Khalil. But revenge is a two-edged weapon, and dangerous to use. You intended to slay the man who insulted you. Even had you suc-ceeded, it would have been an evil thing for Bab-il-Howa, causing punishments and a whole train of fur-ther evils. But you did not shoot the major, Khalil. He left Kfar Shalom after dinner. The jeep you shot at was our own, containing two of our kibbutzniks, and one of them was hit instead."

He paused, and the air was thick with the unan-swered question. Khalil licked dry lips and turned his head slightly to look at Selim and the two Jewish boys. Selim made a small gesture of helpless friendship, but Dan stared miserably at the ground, and Leo, his nar-row jaw set and hard, refused to look at Khalil. A sick feeling growing within him, Khalil turned back to Avram.

"Who is it that I have shot?" he asked steadily, and the words were hard to say.

Avram's eyes were sad and equally steady, looking straight into his. "Even now," he said slowly, "Moshe, who loves thee as a brother, is being rushed to a hospital with a wound in his shoulder and another in his head."

Khalil bowed his head and struggled for self-control, feeling that he was in a dream sent by demons. His lips trembled. He set them tightly together with an effort that caused his throat and jaw to ache. His righteous anger had turned into an evil spirit, lashing out sideways to hurt Khalil by hurting his friend. Of what use was it to Moshe that Khalil had not intended to hurt him? He raised stricken eyes.

"Will he die?"

"The doctor thinks he will live," said Avram gently. "Let us thank God for this."

Khalil drew a quick, shaky breath and braced his shoulders again. "I cannot undo it," he said helplessly. "If I could take the bullets from Moshe into my own body, I would do so. When he is well he shall shoot me in return . . ." His voice trailed off. He knew Moshe would do no such thing. And he could think of nothing else to say.

"My son shall be well punished," said Moussa harshly. "He shall be beaten and then disowned. He has disgraced my name and my village. All who shared in this deed shall suffer, as I promised before. What of the others, Khalil?"

Khalil set his mouth stubbornly. Tale-bearing was for dogs like Jawad, with whom he should never have associated. Besides, he didn't really care whether the others were punished or not.

Not that his silence mattered. Everyone knew. All eyes turned to the three. Jawad looked sullen, Ali hangdog, Hassoun cringed at Moussa's expression.

"It was all Khalil's fault," Jawad muttered.

"Khalil shall be dealt with!" thundered Moussa. "Who art thou, thou cancer in my village, thou yellow dog, to follow the leadership of a boy of twelve? Thou hast been a running sore, an obscene corruption, a creator of violence ever since thy illegal return across the border. Aye, let the Yahud hear; I confess my fault as well, for permitting it." He looked straight at Avram, who showed every sign of being suddenly unable to understand a word of Arabic, and back at Jawad. "I do not excuse my son, but neither do I excuse thee, thou scorpion pig! Son of devils! Hyena! Diseased blot of a weasel! Unclean offspring of snakes and rats!"

His rage was tremendous, his invective awesome. Arabs and Jews alike listened spellbound as it roared and reverberated. Yusif's lips moved in silent repetition. Father was far better than Uncle Rashid, now he came to think of it. He was now including all four culprits in his tirade and seemed about to cast them forth from the village with terrible curses on their heads. That meant Yusif would now be second son instead of third, and no doubt Allah would presently get rid of Ahmed as well.

Moussa finished for the moment and turned back to Avram. "I shall banish them," he said steadily, his head high and his eyes aglitter. "But I, who am mukhtar of this village, am also responsible. I am shamed by this deed. What shall I do to wipe out the debt and restore my honor, oh Mukhtar of Kfar Shalom?"

The air felt like an electric storm. Everyone sensed that this was a critical moment. Avram felt the aching heart and injured pride of the unbending man before him as if it were his own, for he had the gift of compassion, and could not bear to see another person diminished. He longed to clasp Moussa's arms, call him friend, declare the matter forgotten. It would have been a great mistake. Moussa would have taken it either as contemptible weakness or as doubly-humiliating condescension. No, honor must be salvaged by the Arab code of justice and retribution, or this matter would remain a festering wheel of guilt, resentment, grievance, and hatred.

And so Avram took time and thought it over while the village waited. At last he raised his curly brown head and met Moussa's unflinching gaze.

"I have an idea," he said. "It is your right, oh Mukhtar, to banish those who did the deed. But retribution is better than punishment, and justice is better than blind revenge. Revenge and hatred and violence create one another. Let us try to end hatred now."

Moussa nodded, the black burden of shame already lifting slightly. The matter was taking on a new, detached perspective, as a problem in ethics and justice to be settled between mukhtars.

"Let it be thus, if you agree," Avram went on. "Because of these four, Moshe will be unable to work for many weeks. We need his hands, for there is much work to be done in our infant village. Therefore let these help to do his share. Because thy son was ringleader, let him come to live with us in Moshe's place, as Moshe's hands."

"And as hostage," put in Moussa, much struck by the logic and fittingness of this. It was ideal reparation, exactly suited to the offense, and a direct consequence of it. Those who had done the deed would compensate for the results of the deed, and he who was indirectly responsible should suffer by being deprived of the labor and presence of his son. It was a good solution, and one with dignity. He elaborated on it.

"These others, whom you would find a great inconvenience at night, shall come to thee by day and work, as well, and return here to sleep. And if any offend thee or fail to satisfy thee in any way, they shall be banished from Bab-il-Howa after all."

His villagers stared, very much shocked. Their mukhtar should be protesting any punishment, denying everything, complaining that they were all innocent and any retribution much too severe. Had Allah made him mad, to turn against his own people that way? They muttered darkly.

Jawad took courage and raised his voice, puce-faced with his fury. "I will not! Never will I abase myself so! To work for the accursed Yahud! No! I spit on them!"

He looked ready to do so, but then prudently changed his mind and merely made snarling noises to express his hatred and contempt.

"Very well," said Moussa, sounding almost pleased. "I cast thee forth from the village. Thou wilt leave before sunset. Go back to Syria, for there is no place for such as thee in Israel." He stared quellingly at Hassoun and Ali. "What of thee? And Khalil? Will ye join him in exile? Or will ye stay and take the beatings ye have earned and make thy retribution? Speak."

Hassoun, his full lips looking oddly weak and petulant in his sharp-cut face, remained sullen. It was Ali who spoke. "I will stay and accept punishment, oh Mukhtar, but do not cast me out." Hassoun shrugged, dropped his eyes from Moussa's steady gaze, and nodded.

Khalil felt his own shame doubled for having associated with them. His lips thin and tight lest they tremble, he looked at Avram. In an odd manner, the only way he could keep any self-respect at all was to cast all his pride underfoot and trample it himself. "I will make full recompense—if I can," he said in a low voice.

"Good," said Avram, as man-to-man, and then mercifully shifted the attention away from him. "There is another problem, oh Mukhtar. When the doctor came to tend Moshe, bringing Major Schorr back, they wanted to know what happened."

Slowly this sank in. The villagers realized that this

morning's work might cost them their homes and village. It had never seemed a real threat before, but now it did. Moussa's madness was now clear, for it was necessary that he pacify Authority. Eyes that had been staring at him and the Yahud with resentment now turned with greater resentment toward the miscreants.

Khalil scarcely noticed, for he was past caring what the villagers thought. He swallowed. His eyes pleaded against his will. "What—did you tell them?"

Avram seemed to be speaking to Khalil and Moussa alone. "We told them lies," he said. "We said that it was a border skirmish on top of the hill. I think Major Schorr doesn't believe it, for he gave me a very suspicious look, but we all swore to it and he cannot prove otherwise."

Moussa stood still considering this and its implications. Khalil spoke, bewilderment crowding all else from his mind. It was clear from their faces that Leo and Dan were feeling no great friendship toward him.

"Why?" he demanded urgently, and all leaned forward to hear the answer.

Avram hesitated, picking his words. "Why should all be uprooted from their homes for the fault of a few?" he asked, and then grinned suddenly. "Besides, I do not like the Major very much, myself. But," he added, grave again, "we shall have to walk on eggs from now on. He will be watching like a stalking lion, and will pounce at the smallest reason, and then"—he shrugged —"too bad . . . But we will intrude no longer on thy village, oh Moussa. Let us take our leave. You shall send Khalil and the others to us when you will."

Moussa nodded with dignity untouched by the last hour. Khalil, numb almost to the point of indifference, stood staring at nothing at all. Silence radiated over the murmuring village when the Yahud had left, causing the crowd to melt away very quietly, with uneasy side glances at the mukhtar. Kbeer Abou spoke at last, in a burst of indignation. Something had just dawned on him.

"If thy son goes to stay in that Yahud village," he demanded, "how can any attack it for fear of harming him?"

Moussa's smile was without mirth. "They cannot, oh father of my second wife. Remember it well."

14. the hostage

Khalil walked down the hill to Kfar Shalom with his shoulders back and his head high. Pride was his refuge —pride that he came freely to make recompense, to restore his honor and that of his father. And pride would keep him here far more surely than bars or chains.

Hassoun and Ali scuffled sullenly behind. "Art thou eager for punishment, oh son of the mukhtar, that you go to it so quickly?"

Khalil didn't turn his head. They had no pride. And he *was* in a hurry—to have the dreaded arrival over. Better to go meet a thing than to wait for it! How would they act, these Yahud almost-friends whom he had visited and then harmed? He very much hoped that they wouldn't affront his self-respect with kindness.

He took a deep breath as they reached the carob tree, and only a very sharp eye could have seen the taut muscles beneath the calm of his face. Chaim saw him first, and gave a curt nod.

"Shalom," he said rather shortly. "I'll get Avram."
He vanished, and although Khalil had not expected or
wanted friendliness, there was a lump in his throat,
and his sharp chin lifted another quarter inch.

"Salaam, Khalil," said Avram's voice matter-of-factly
a moment later. "Salaam, Hassoun and Ali. Chaim,
will you take these two over to the barn and let them
start helping? I'll show Khalil his bed first." He led the
way into the long wooden dormitory with a row of
straw mattresses on rough wooden frames. Everything,
Moshe had explained earlier, was primitive and make-
shift for the moment, but they would begin to improve
living conditions during the winter. The thought of
Moshe's bright grin was a pain. Khalil stood staring
at his bed for a moment, and then turned abruptly to
Avram.

"Does he know? Does he know what—who—"

"Not yet," said Avram. "Not about you. He is not
well enough yet to be told anything. When the time
comes—Would you rather tell him yourself?"

Khalil jerked his head in a way that might have
meant anything. He wasn't sure himself what it meant.

"Come along," said Avram, not pressing the point.
"You can help Dan with the irrigation."

By the time the sun was low and Hassoun and Ali
had headed glumly back to Bab-il-Howa, Khalil was
very tired. Irrigating was hard work; much harder
than watching goats, though he didn't quite venture to
say so. Dan had lost his slow, amiable grin, and had as

little to do with Khalil as possible. Leo glowered, and some of the others looked through him altogether. Khalil bore it without anger, for it was just.

It was nearly dark when they trudged back to the main building, where a girl's voice hailed them just outside a storage shed. "Just what I wanted! Men! With strong arms! Will you help take some of this stuff to the kitchen?"

A flashlight flickered inside the shed on some bulky sacks—perhaps of potatoes. The slim figure of Chava stood panting over one, and Chaim clucked reprovingly. "You needn't think you can do *everything* a man can," he teased her, and then switched to Arabic for Khalil's benefit. "Let's carry these to the kitchen."

Khalil looked at the sacks and at Chava, and stiffened. "Women's work is for women!" he snapped, deeply insulted. "You are just trying to humiliate me! I will not do it!"

Chava turned on him furiously. "And I suppose men's work is shooting your friends from ambush!" she blazed. "Well, I don't want your help, you maskin, you viper, you father of treachery! Get out!"

"Hey!" began Chaim, and was interrupted by Avram's deep voice.

"What's all this?"

Everyone tried to tell him at once. Chava fairly sputtered with rage, so that it was a full two minutes before Avram could get it straight. "All right," he said. "Chava, take that chip off your shoulder and calm down. Go on back to the kitchen, and we'll bring the stuff."

She went, still fuming, and Avram turned to Khalil. "It's all right," he said. "No one is trying to humiliate you. You are in our village now, and must try to understand our customs. There is no work here that is disgraceful for a man to do. We share work alike, men and women, except that some things require the strong muscles of a man, and we men do those jobs. That's all. Come on, now, let's get these into the kitchen, or we won't have any dinner tonight."

He picked up the largest sack and headed out the door without even a backward look to see what Khalil would do. Chaim took another and followed. And Khalil, after hesitating a moment, took the third. He didn't like it—but if Avram, the mukhtar, could do it, he supposed he could, too.

He had never been in the kitchen before. There was a large stove at one end, the like of which Khalil had never seen before, where men and girls together did fragrant things with food. Chaim and Avram put down their sacks, and were laughing and bantering with Dan and a tawny-haired girl named Judy who had just come in from the fields. Chaim tried to sample something from a large pot and a girl rapped his knuckles smartly. Khalil stared, scandalized, and Chaim, sucking his knuckles, grinned.

"Shalom, Khalil!" chirped Judy, with the genuine smile of someone who hadn't the faintest idea how to hold a grudge. Though she was only a female, it was as a drink of cool water to Khalil, and he smiled back.

A feminine voice called through from the dining room, and Dan went obediently in to help move a large table. Khalil watched disapprovingly, and then let his eyes circle the kitchen. Leo was stirring something on the stove with the air of a professional. Avram and a girl emptied the disputed sacks into a barrel. Chava, atop a stool, was reaching for something on a top shelf, but with her small aggressive chin turned slightly over her shoulder, and one brown eye fixed on Khalil with bright hostility. Clearly she was itching for another round with him, waiting for the chance to pounce. And although Khalil had several points he wished to make clear to that little she-devil, he did not feel that this was the appropriate time or place. He felt suddenly bewildered and in a dream, and was glad enough to stretch himself later on that strange bed so far from the floor, between Leo and Dan.

Then, of course, he lay awake, ill at ease on his high mattress, unable to stop thinking. It was all more strange than he had realized. Male and female eating together at high tables . . . sitting around afterwards, talking, singing, dancing a wild circular dance that got faster and faster and then suddenly broke to pieces, laughing, while a girl with golden hair began to do weird foreign dancing called ballet. Someone actually sat reading a book, and a man was darning his own shirt. And—strangest of all amid all the other strangeness—the familiar sight of a chessboard, but with two girls' heads bent tautly over it!

Khalil had blinked and stared, alternately, while staccato Hebrew rattled around him. Sometimes those who spoke Arabic kindly translated for him, but on that first night and for several to follow, it was kindness almost wasted. He was as a porcupine in a nest of mongooses, prickly and uncomfortable, walking in the midst of a strained silence. Only Judy and Avram and Shari managed to be at ease with him. Some didn't try, but stared at him with hard, angry eyes, or looked through him as if he didn't exist. Khalil reminded himself that this was just—but he began to chafe under it. Was he a dog to be so treated?

And then, within a week, things improved. The good will of the kibbutz expanded to take him in; and he began to feel less alien and more used to the strange ways of Yahud. Presently the only ones who still treated him coldly were Dan and Leo, Chava, and Malkah—kibbutz nurse and Moshe's future wife who, not unnaturally, was very much annoyed at Khalil.

Three of these four were cornered one morning by the washstands by Judy and Shari, who looked fierce and determined. Shari seemed quite ready to go bang, and even Judy's merry face was stern.

"You're not being fair to Khalil!" she announced, going straight to the heart of the matter.

Dan looked miserable. Leo and Chava exploded in unison. "Fair to *him!* I like that! I suppose he was fair to Moshe! I suppose Moshe just loved being nearly killed from ambush by a little sneaking beast whom he'd befriended!"

"Don't be silly," retorted Judy calmly. "You know perfectly well Khalil wouldn't have hurt Moshe for the world. He thought it was Major Schorr in the jeep."

"I suppose that's all right?" sneered Leo. "It's a dirty Arab trick, attacking from ambush, and you know it."

Shari at once went bang. "I suppose you never did anything dirty or sneaky in your life?" she demanded scathingly. "What about the time—"

"Shut up," said Judy. "Both of you." And such was the force of her personality that they both closed their mouths and contented themselves with glaring at each other.

"Put yourself in his place," urged Judy. "You know as well as I do that he didn't see anything wrong in it. They have different rules. They thought we cheated horribly during the war because we didn't wait for dawn to attack, remember? Anyhow, I thought the whole idea of having him come here was so that he could find out that we're really pretty nice and vice versa. So let's give it a chance. He's worth having for a friend, and I think you know it."

Chava, arms folded and one narrow foot tapping in a militant way, shook her head. "It isn't that," she said. "I grew up among Arabs, and I know there are different standards, and I like Selim, and Jasmin's a perfect darling. But Khalil's one of the sort I hate; an arrogant beast. Besides, how do you think Moshe will feel about us being chaverim with the boy who ambushed and nearly killed him?"

Judy looked throughtful. "I don't know exactly," she confessed. "But I do know what he said when Avram and I went in to visit him yesterday, and Avram told him what happened."

"What?" they demanded, the argument almost forgotten.

Judy's eyes danced. "When he got to the bit about Khalil thinking it was Major Schorr and shooting, Moshe said, 'Nice try!' "

Leo grinned reluctantly, Shari giggled, even Chava chuckled. Only Dan, who loathed violence, looked pained.

"So if Moshe doesn't hold a grudge, why should we?" persisted Judy. "Dan, I'm surprised at you. Hating's a kind of violence, you know."

Dan looked sheepish, nodded, turned, and went out to look at his precious trees. On the way, he managed to find Khalil and wish him good morning.

Leo scowled for a moment, then sighed and shrugged. "All right, all right; stop nagging, you females! I'll make up with Khalil—but I'll do it my own way." And he stalked off, contriving to look as if he'd won the argument.

Chava laughed suddenly. "Oh well, I'll give him a chance to redeem himself. But I won't put up with any of that masculine superiority bit, I warn you! I'd just love to prove to that young pup that women are really much superior!"

"So we are," agreed Judy modestly. "But who needs to prove it?"

That evening when Kfar Shalom gathered for dinner, Leo and Khalil appeared together. They were both considerably battered and bruised, and they looked outrageously pleased with themselves. The kibbutz regarded them with deep interest.

"Must have been some fight," said tall Yaacov admiringly.

Khalil went to sleep that night sore in body but elated. It wasn't merely the fact that he and Leo were friends again, or that he had somehow been accepted in the kibbutz. There was something else, which was balm to his bruised pride, which he couldn't put in words. It was the fact that Leo had challenged him as an equal, they had fought as equals, and they had shaken hands afterwards man to man.

15. the lull

All day and night lightning had played among the hills of Upper Galilee, almost as if Allah had decided to play an accompaniment to the crisis boiling in the small village below. Then rain fell, drenching and torrential, beating in thunder upon the flat-roofed houses, sluicing down the thick yellow-gray walls, soaking into the parched earth and rushing down the central gutter of the street, carrying the evil-smelling refuse with it, so that for the first time since spring there was no stench.

Jawad had gone back across the border; Khalil and his sore back were recovering honor in the Yahud village; Hassoun and Ali worked out their penance daily, returning each evening subdued and untalkative. A kind of exhausted peace fell over Bab-il-Howa. In the dimly lit house at the top of the street, Moussa and Ahmed sat after dinner with a flickering oil lamp between them, refitting the plow and yoke for the winter planting. Kbeer Abou sat apart, smoking his water pipe in a silence which might be either sulky or meditative. Across the room, near the small stove, Hayat tended her baby, while Zubaida and Jasmin knelt on either side of a small tripod, swinging a goatskin of milk monotonously back and forth between them. The resulting butter would be slightly goat-flavored, but as no one had ever tasted any other kind of butter, this was never noticed.

Ahmed's strong, quiet hands worked in efficient silence on the wooden yoke, and his mind was on the land. Would the rain soften it far down, so that the plow would cut deeply this year, or would more of the soil be washed away, and the crops be poorer than ever? He kept wishing he could talk to the yellow-haired Yahudi Dan about it . . .

Moussa took quiet comfort in his eldest son these days. Ahmed was almost a man, now: steady, responsible, obedient. It was true that he somewhat lacked Khalil's fire, but Moussa had had quite enough of fire for a while. Stability was better. Zubaida was a comfort, too. She was a good and wise wife and mother, and it was not her fault that Jasmin and Khalil had both misbehaved these last months.

Perhaps, he decided, it was no one's fault, but that of the times. Avram was a good man even by Arab standards. It was just that the two ways of life did not mix. Every contact brought trouble or evil. He stared unseeing at the goad in his hands. No, it would not do. Contact must cease as soon as Khalil returned with the debt canceled. Oh, there would be good will, of course,

and perhaps an occasional visit between himself and
Avram, but no more. His village must be protected
from dangerous new ideas. As it was, he was not at all
sure that Jasmin had not suffered from the sight of
Yahud women. There was something about her lately
—something questioning, independent, unfeminine . . .

Jasmin, as if attracted by her father's attention,
turned her head and met his eyes. And instead of lowering her own, she remained gazing at him with a level,
appraising look not at all becoming a daughter. Annoyed, Moussa beetled his brows at her in a piercing
stare intended to chasten her. Jasmin beetled her own
in a comical duplication which neither of them realized, and it became almost a staring contest. Identical
pride and stubbornness caused both jaws to jut slightly
forward, even while both pairs of hands continued at
their tasks. The tension built up, and Moussa's face
began to darken at such insolence. Zubaida trembled.

"Jasmin!" she said sharply.

Jasmin looked at her, half glad and half sorry. Her
heart was beating rapidly at her own temerity, but she
knew somehow that the thing which had been building
up was not ended, but only postponed. She threw her
mother a look of apology and resentment mixed, and
lowered her eyes with a small sigh to the goatskin
swinging to and fro between them.

Back and forth, over and over, a symbol of a woman's
life, endlessly dull and monotonous and drab. There

would be no school for her, no hope of escape, and lately she was also deprived of her visits to Kfar Shalom now that Khalil was there. Even when he returned, it was only a matter of time before she was found out, and punished, and prevented from ever going again.

It wasn't fair! Why should women be treated as slaves, prisoners, animals? She had always been told that this was Allah's law, a fact of life, no more to be questioned than the seasons. But it wasn't! Surely Allah created all, even Infidels and Unbelievers. And the Yahud didn't recognize this law—and they weren't punished for it—and their women bloomed and were happy and equal. How could this be? How could people who believed in a false god, who denied Allah's laws, be allowed to go on thriving? Was it possible—

Was it possible that Qassab al-Sayid had not gone far enough in his remarks about Allah's Will? Was it possible that Allah did not consider females inferior—*and never had?*

The idea leaped into the center of her mind with an explosion like a million little lights. It was all a lie! A lie that had been going on for unknown hundreds of years, generation after generation of women suffering from it, generations of idle, selfish, arrogant men taking advantage! It *must* be true! That was why Allah had permitted the Yahud to win the war! He wasn't a mean, unfair God at all; it was men! Perhaps, she decided defiantly, it was The Prophet, as well. He was a man, wasn't he?

She shivered a little with shock and excitement. Her eyes—enormous—were fixed on something quite outside the house. Unconsciously her slender back straightened and her chin lifted.

Zubaida, watching her, shivered as well, and a vehement appeal for help went flying heavenward.

It was not easy for a new idea to enter the slow and methodical mind of Ahmed, but occasionally it happened, and when it did, there was no way out. On these rare times, it would sit there for some time, alien and ignored. Presently, when it did not go away, Ahmed would begin to eye it with wary curiosity, and then to turn it over and examine it with great caution. If it did not fall apart under this prodding, it could begin slowly to make itself at home, until one day Ahmed would decide to adopt it—to the great astonishment of his family.

The idea of going over to visit the village of his yellow-haired friend, to see how they farmed there, had been settling down for some time now. On a day when the rain had stopped for the moment, and the sky was wearing the pale blue of winter, Ahmed quietly put his warmest aba over his striped tob and walked over to Kfar Shalom.

He was not there very long, really, but he emerged looking dazed. He had greeted his brother briefly, and then vanished into a long conversation with Dan and two Yahud who spoke Arabic fluently. They had looked at gardens and baby orchards, machines, and irrigation ditches, had talked of terracing, and ferti- lizers, and drainage, and enrichment and conservation of soil. The rather bare but orderly storehouse of Ahmed's mind was a perfect chaos of new ideas all jumbling against one another, and each clamoring for attention. It was the most unsettling thing that had ever happened to him, and he had a vague feeling that he would never be quite the same again.

He went home as quietly as he had left, and took up the wooden yoke he had been making. He looked at it thoughtfully. There was no special expression on his face, but Zubaida lifted her head with a mother's sixth sense, and regarded him closely. Ahmed looked, she decided, as if he had a touch of indigestion. And in this she was very close to the truth.

Yusif's mind was quite different from Ahmed's. No leisurely storehouse of ideas there, but a short, direct passage leading from impulse to action, and the sim- pler and more direct, the better. It was a rare occasion that found Yusif at a loss in this regard. But the rare occasion had been upon him since the day of Khalil's disgrace. A new sun had burst in Yusif's sky that day, and he did not know what to do about it.

It had started when the two Yahud boys stood out- side the house waiting for Father and Avram to come out. Yusif, deeply curious about these aliens, had come to stare—and he had found himself fascinated by the tall dark one, with the narrow face and shock of black wavy hair.

Yusif went on staring, until the intensity of his interest drew Leo's attention from the crisis. He looked down. Round black eyes in a round face stared at him unwinkingly, the mouth a small round "o" of deep concentration. Funny little thing, thought Leo, and smiled.

Now, Leo's smile was a remarkable affair. It began at the corners of his eyes and crinkled his lean face in a warm, magnetic radiance. It caused people to love him instantly. And Yusif, receiving its full impact, was at once smitten with hero-worship.

Here was a man worthy of his admiration, doubtless a perfect terror of a warrior, a fellow of fire and brilliance! That he was a Yahudi was of no importance: such minor details could be left to Allah to correct some day when He wasn't busy. Yusif remained rooted, staring, nothing whatever showing on his face.

Leo, having no suspicion of his own impact on the little fellow, merely found the relentless stare a trifle disconcerting. He smiled now and then when he happened to look that way, but when Avram and Moussa emerged he at once forgot all about Yusif.

But Yusif didn't forget. He merely didn't know what to do about it, until, eventually, it occurred to him that if he went to the Yahud village he might see his hero again. His channels of impulse being in good working order, he went.

If his heart quaked just a trifle, his small impassive face never showed it. He stood at the pine grove with great dignity, wondering what to do next, until a Yahuda with shorts and black hair came up and addressed him in Arabic.

"A thousand welcomes," she said politely. "Hast thou come to honor us with a visit?"

Yusif swelled a little with importance. This was the way the son of the mukhtar and a great warrior liked to be treated. "Peace be upon you," he said majestically. "I seek the Yahud whose smile is as the sun."

It did not take Shari long to decide whom Yusif meant. She had known Leo for two and a half years now, and one of the most infuriating things about him was the way he used that smile to captivate people.

"Perhaps I know the one you mean," she said with a wry smile, and led Yusif to the still-new and scrupulously clean cow barn. Leo, busy cleaning it out, looked up in surprise.

"I think you have another admirer, oh Great One," murmured Shari with a bantering mockery that was not lost on Yusif. His wonder increased. Did the Yahuda dare take such liberties with his hero? She must also be a great one! He deigned to smile graciously at Shari before setting about the business of getting properly acquainted with Leo.

Thereafter Yusif skipped Mahmoud's school more often than not in order to go visit Leo, while Ahmed, glutted though he was with undigested ideas, went back almost daily for more. Jasmin seethed quietly, full-scale rebellion fermenting within her, while her twin began to settle in and feel almost at home amid the enemy aliens.

And Moussa, struggling with plans to preserve his village from the infestations of strange new ways, for once failed to see what was going on under his nose.

16. selim

Selim was finding it a long and lonely rainy season. He missed Khalil badly, and he also missed his new friends at Kfar Shalom. But he felt strongly that it would be better if he did not go visit them just now. So he tried to busy himself helping his father and brothers with winter repairs, and he took long walks in the hills, and he and his father had many talks about going to train to become a teacher, and when and how to get the mukhtar's approval.

At other times he studied the book which he had borrowed from Malkah, and he thought about things. He thought about Khalil, and about the two villages which were neighbors but not quite friends, and also about the continuing border troubles, and about certain stealthy sounds in Bab-il-Howa at nights. And he thought about Jasmin, and wondered how it felt to be a bird in a cage.

He was sitting on the doorstep of his home on a mild day, with his borrowed book before him, when he felt a small presence, and turned to see his sister Katan star-

ing over his shoulder with wonder. He smiled, and
moved over to make room for her beside him. She
snuggled against his arm—for there was great love between them—her eyes still on his book. "What does it
say?" she asked.

"It says many wise things," Selim told her, turning
pages to find something that a seven-year-old might
understand. "It says that love gives itself, and that
when you love you should not think that Allah is in
your heart, but that you are in the heart of Allah. Do
you understand that, Katan?"

She rested dark head against his shoulder for a moment, and then nodded. "Yes. But I don't understand
how you find the words in those funny squiggly marks.
Is it magic? I wish—"

Selim completed her wish in his mind. Of course!
She was like Jasmin! And she could easily become just
as unhappy, fretting behind bars of ignorance and restrictions. Surely it wasn't necessary! Moshe had told
him that in the towns many Arab girls went to school,
and had done so for years, even before Palestine became Israel. Now Israel wanted to extend this opportunity to all children. Perhaps there was hope, then,
for Katan . . .

"You would like to learn to read, wouldn't you?" he
mused.

Katan stiffened. Selim looked down at her and was
startled. Her face was as awed and shining as if she had
just glimpsed Paradise and couldn't believe it was for

her. "Are you teasing me, Selim?" she whispered. "It would not be ipe for a girl to learn?"

Selim thought quickly, and in dismay. What had he done? Could he open a door and then slam it in her face? Could he teach her himself? Would it be right? Another look at Katan's face, and he didn't care if it was right or not.

"I'll try to teach thee, Katan," he said softly. "But it must be a secret between us. Do you understand?"

She peered up at him wisely, almost with amusement. "Of course!" she whispered with a vigorous nod. "I'll never say a *word*, not even after I've learned to read better than Yusif! He is lazy," she confided with scorn. "He creeps away to visit the Yahud village when he should be at school, and only a fool would stay away from school when he is permitted to go!" In her voice was the angry frustration of a starving man watching another fling food into the sea. Selim, very much moved, was ashamed that he hadn't noticed before.

"All right," he said, and picked up the bit of sacking which *would* slide off the dark curls. "Mother doesn't need you now? Then we'll go up to the threshing floor and have the first lesson." And he took her warm small hand in his and stood up.

As they passed the spring, there was a small huddle of older girls, Jasmin in the middle. She looked angry, desolate, defiant—and also, somehow furtive.

"What's wrong with Jasmin?" Selim asked worriedly, and then blinked at his sister's reproachful stare. "I mean especially now," he amended humbly. The stare went on. "Oh," he said feebly, realizing. Of course! She, too, was deprived of her visits to Kfar Shalom, and it was worse for her. She had nothing else. If only—

"I *do* wish you could teach Jasmin, too," sighed Katan, satisfied now that her obtuse brother finally understood without any pledges of silence being broken.

Selim nodded his head and then shook it. Impossible, of course. It was erratic but not improper for him to go off alone with Katan, who was a very small girl and his sister. Jasmin was neither. He considered the problem. "Perhaps you can teach her everything I teach you?"

Katan's round eyes became perfect circles. "Me? Teach a big girl? Teach *Jasmin?* I couldn't!"

"If Jasmin cares about learning, she won't care who teaches her," Selim said firmly. "And you'll learn all the better, yourself, that way. At least ask her, Katan."

Katan nodded with the air of one who has just consented to run the universe for a while and plans to do her very best. "And now teach me some words!" she commanded, hugging her mantle closely against the wind.

"Not yet." Selim became all teacher. Odd how strongly he felt he would be good at it! He smoothed a bit of ground and found a pointed stone. "First you must learn letters. You see, letters are marks that stand for sounds, and when you put sounds together, you get words. There aren't very many sounds, and when you have learned the letters for all of them, then you will be able to read any word you see."

And he began to draw the complex flowing lines of the first Arabic letter.

Jasmin avidly picked Katan's brain of everything Selim put there—and was not satisfied. A few months ago—even a few weeks ago—she would have been delighted. Now her discontent had passed the point of being happy with crumbs: she wanted the whole loaf. Selim, puzzled by the continuing scowl on her face, might have understood better if he had ever studied the history of revolutions, where people begin by wanting only enough to eat, and end by demanding to run the whole country themselves. Not having learned any history, Selim fell back on his understanding of people, which was not a bad substitute in this case. He watched with mixed approval and alarm while Jasmin proceeded to spread discontent and the alphabet among the girls of Bab-il-Howa.

More clusters of girls' heads began to appear, inside houses on rainy days, around smooth patches of ground on fine ones. They muttered earnestly at each other and drew letters in what Selim considered to be the most reckless fashion.

"Tell them to be careful!" he warned Katan urgently. "I can't think why no one has noticed yet that something is going on!"

Katan dimpled at him. "Men never notice what female children do," she pointed out wisely. "And the mothers just think it's new games. And no one would dare tell, not even Nejmi, however jealous she is of Jasmin, for she'd be punished herself for going on listening and not saying anything sooner."

Selim shook his head wonderingly at this glimpse into the feminine world. No doubt it would be very useful when he became a teacher. But he began to worry about what he had so innocently started. It threatened to get out of hand, and the consequences might be very explosive indeed—especially with so many other currents still sizzling through the village.

Only yesterday the still-suspicious Major Schorr had paid another visit to the village, and had as usual left behind a mutter of maledictions. He never found anything—but Selim was uneasy. There were things going on at night, and they centered around Hassoun. He felt sure of it.

And what if he was adding to the tension in the village in a way that might have evil results for everyone?

He took his troubles to his father, who knew and approved Katan's reading lessons. A modern-minded man, Kassem just chuckled at the thought of all the village girls indulging in subversive activities, and refused to take it seriously.

Mahmoud the imam was much more helpful. He listened attentively, fingering his white beard, and then sat thinking for a moment.

"The world we pass through is a troubled wilderness," he observed at last. "How shall any of us avoid committing evil in some form? When we eat mutton, it gives life and strength to our bodies, but does it benefit the sheep? We can only follow paths of true unselfishness and good will, and leave the consequences to Allah. Pray for wisdom and follow it, even though apparent evil may come of thy best intent . . . And if trouble comes to thee, come to me for support," he added with a smile.

Selim walked back down the street elatedly. It was good to have the imam's approval. So good did he feel that when he met Ali coming back from his daily work at Kfar Shalom, he gave him an unusually friendly smile. "Salaam, Ali. How is it with thee?"

Ali stopped. Words poured out. "It is very strange with me, oh Selim!" he announced plaintively. "I do not know what to believe or think about the Yahud! They do strange things and have strange ways, and I find that I like them against my will, even while I dislike them. Hassoun says I am being misled by demons, yet the mukhtar sends us there to work with these Unbelievers. How am I to know what to think?"

"Talk to Mahmoud," Selim advised him sagely. "Believe what he tells thee, Ali."

Ali, who needed to be told what to think, looked relieved. "I will do so," he said, starting on up the hill. Then he turned and looked over his shoulder at Selim.

"I think thy best friend is thine no longer," he announced with a touch of his old malice. "Khalil begins to live and talk like a Yahudi. He learns their language and wears their clothing, and is great friends with the one called Lee-o. He will no longer wish thy friendship after this."

Selim stood thinking for some minutes after Ali had vanished around the sharp bend. He was not worried about Khalil's friendship. It was good news Ali had brought—if it was true. Perhaps now was the time to go back for another visit to Kfar Shalom. He started on toward his home. Yes, it was the time. He would also return the borrowed book, and ask Malkah if she had one that would be suitable for Katan. Tomorrow he would go.

It was a bright cold day, with a sharp wind sweeping over the hills and down the valley. Selim wrapped his heavy aba about him closely as he walked through the pine grove and up to the main building. No one was outside, but sounds came from the kitchen, followed by laughter, scuffling, and then Chaim, a pan, and Chava.

Selim ducked, Chaim vanished, laughing, and Chava stood in the doorway of the kitchen, making threatening noises after him. Then she saw Selim, and her face broke into welcome. "Salaam, salaam! We have missed thee, Selim! Why have you stayed away so long? Avram, Mia, Dina! Look who's here! Why *did* you stay away, Selim?"

"I thought it would be better if I did not come for a

while," he told her simply, and she frowned for a moment.

"Yes, I suppose you were right," she conceded. "Do you want to see Khalil?"

Selim looked at Avram, who was shaking his hand warmly. "If— When he is not busy," he said. "May I? Is all well with thy village? What of Moshe?"

It was like coming to a second home. They were all glad to see him; they promised to get him brightly colored books with large print and gay pictures for Katan, and gave him much delighted encouragement. It was indeed all well with Khalil, who was clearly finding himself in a new way here, and no longer very much at war with himself. And Moshe had come back from the city hospital, thin, heavily bandaged, but as cheerful and cocky as ever; and all was very well indeed between him and Khalil.

"I told him next time he goes for the major, I'll help," grinned Moshe. "Only let's be sure it's Schorr we get, and not some nice innocent kid like me!"

17. kfar shalom

Winter moved along. Icy blasts swept the hills now and then, and the air was brightly cold. Mountains to the north were snow-covered. At Kfar Shalom, Moshe was by now an impatient convalescent, and Khalil a part of the family. So, almost, were Selim, Yusif, and Ahmed, who were careful never to mention that the mukhtar knew nothing of all these visits, and also careful never to be seen by Hassoun or Ali.

"You've never once gone up to visit your father," Leo observed to Khalil wonderingly. He still missed his own dead parents badly. "Why not?"

Khalil just shook his head. He wouldn't dream of returning until it was with honor fully restored and he could go proudly, the son of the mukhtar, free from shame and obligation.

One afternoon Malkah met Selim with the news that the books for Katan had arrived, and the next day Selim brought his little sister to get them. She stared in wonder at all the strange new things, and let loose a spate of eager questions that caused him to appeal to Chava for help. For Katan was too young to think that a thing was wrong because it was different; she was merely interested and delighted.

Something began to dawn on Selim. "If Arab and Yahud children could know each other's ways and play together when they are young," he told Chava with sudden conviction, "there would be no troubles between us, soon. No one would hate each other."

Chava nodded. "That's what we hope will happen," she said. "Come, Katan, would you like to see the books we have for you, and perhaps read a little for me?"

Katan regarded her gravely, then smiled, and slipped her hand trustingly into the dark one held out to her. Presently, in a corner of the big dining-and-recreation room, she was reading aloud from an enchanting tale of djinni and magic, quite astonishing Chava with her progress, her clear young voice fluting clearly through the closed door—where Yusif was just passing on his way to favor Leo with a visit.

He stopped and listened, nonplussed. But that was Katan's voice! How could she be here? He at once opened the door and stood there, unnoticed, his round face blank with outraged disbelief. Katan *was* here! Katan, moreover, was unmistakably reading! He would not admit even to himself that she was reading better than he could; it was enough that she read at all.

"Katan!" he yelped furiously. "Wicked, shameless girl! What are you doing here? How dare you?"

She jerked her curly head in his direction, and then pressed closer to Chava, who turned ominous brown eyes upon this spoiled brat and waited to see what he would do. Katan took a deep breath.

"I am reading," she told Yusif triumphantly.

"Girls can't read!" he pronounced, swaggering over to glare at the brightly illustrated little book. How very interesting it looked! "You have just been making up stories and pretending to read them!" he discovered with relief.

"I haven't!" cried Katan, stung. "I *can* read, can't I, Chava? I can read better than you, oh stupid Yusif!" And picking up the book, she came much closer to proving it than Yusif could bear. It was too much! He was a mighty warrior, a masterful male, not to be humiliated in this fashion! Behaving as he felt a mighty warrior should, he raised an infuriated arm immediately and silenced Katan by a masterful slap in the face.

Katan squeaked and dropped the book. Then, before either Chava or Yusif could move, nature overcame training, and Katan slapped him back.

The unexpectedness of this second affront robbed Yusif of all power of movement for a second. Then with a screech of rage he moved forward to discipline this daughter of Shaitan—only to find his wrists captured and held by the tall dark Yahuda.

"Let go!" he fumed, twisting and jerking. "How *dare* you! I am the son of the mukhtar and a great

warrior, and I shall punish that Bedouine as she de-
serves!" He bit Chava's hand.

"Ouch!" she yelped. "Thou art a naughty, spoiled,
arrogant little boy, that's what you are! And what is
more, I am going to punish you as *you* deserve!"

Slender though she was, Chava was extremely
strong. Sitting down, she turned the struggling and
yelping Yusif over her knee and applied punishment
in the spot that Allah had thoughtfully provided for it.
She had been itching to do this ever since Yusif began
visiting Kfar Shalom, and she found it a great satisfaction. So did the open-mouthed Katan!

When Chava had finished, she held Yusif in place
for a moment and spoke. "Now," she said, "when I let
you up, either you are going to behave in a gentle-
manly fashion as the son of the mukhtar should, or I
shall chastise thee all over again."

She let go, and Yusif bounded away, rubbing the
spot that hurt, glaring at Chava with hatred and morti-
fication—and considerable respect.

Chava smiled at him. "Already this is over and forgotten in my mind," she informed him casually.
"Nothing at all has happened between us. I see that
thou art a good and brave boy, a worthy son of a mukhtar; and I would like to be friends with thee."

Yusif's glare faded slowly. It occurred to him that,
female or no, this was a person after his own heart; one
who put thought into action with no delay whatever.
Moreover, she was very strong indeed!

"Bismallah!" he said in awe. "It is a pity thou art not a man, for I think you would be a very great warrior." He thought about this for a moment, and then reached a conclusion which greatly soothed his pride. "I think Allah intended thee for a man, and accidentally put a man's soul into a woman's body. All is forgotten, Man-woman, and I will be friends with thee—but you must never do such a thing again!" he added with severity.

"I am sure there will never be need," she returned gravely, and they shook hands. Then Yusif swaggered out with dignity unimpaired—and the moment the door closed behind him, Chava and Katan became aware of an audience in the kitchen doorway.

They turned. There stood Selim and Khalil, their faces masking a great many mixed emotions.

"How long have you been there?" demanded Chava.

"Since Yusif came in," replied Selim. His eyes sparkled with enjoyment. But it wasn't Selim that worried Chava. She looked at Khalil.

"Oh dear!" she said, to his surprise. "I had no right, did I?—even though he did deserve it. I suppose you'll never forgive me?"

Her genuine regret disarmed Khalil in spite of himself. "It is true that you had no right to strike my brother," he began sternly, and then thawed. "But it was probably good for him."

Chava looked so relieved that he melted still more. "Yusif thinks too much of his own importance," he admitted. "He is liable to grow up just like his grandfather if we don't spank him more often. I forgive thee, Chava."

Chava blinked, unable to decide whether his eyes were twinkling or not. "But if he complains to your father—" she began.

Khalil grinned outright. "I don't think Yusif will mention it to anyone," he predicted with certainty. "He may, presently, tell a story of having conquered all of Kfar Shalom single-handedly, but no one will pay any attention to that."

He expanded his grin to take in Katan, who smiled back tremulously. Everything had been bewildering for a moment, but now it was all right. The wonderful and lordly Khalil was not angry, after all.

"Will you be coming home soon?" she asked him, raising eyes that held an expression very much like that of Yusif toward Leo. Khalil, who had never much noticed Selim's little sister, was startled and touched. What had he ever done to deserve such transparent devotion? He responded with a smile of sweetness that quite startled Chava, and caused Katan's face to light up like candles.

"Soon," he replied. "Moshe is almost well. When he can work as well as before, I shall come home."

They began to move toward the door, for it was time for Selim and Katan to go home. Katan was clutching her precious book, her other hand clasping that of her new friend Chava, but her eyes were still fixed on Khalil.

"You read very well," he told her, causing her cup of joy to overflow. "Soon you will be able to go to school and learn more."

Her eyes widened. She shook her head gently. "Oh, no," she explained, surprised that he should not know this basic fact of life. "School isn't for girls."

"But it will be!" Khalil surprised even himself with his own forcefulness. "Yahud girls go to school, and learn all that boys do. Are Arab girls less than they?" He glared. "Who dares to say our girls are inferior, unworthy of education, condemned to be ignorant among a nation of educated?"

He was standing beneath the carob tree now, nearly shouting. Selim watched with deep interest and growing satisfaction. Something very exciting was happening to Khalil. He had found the kind of battle that just exactly suited him, and could now stop fighting himself and the Yahud. He grinned happily.

"No need to make a speech at us," he pointed out. "Katan and I agree with you. How about convincing people like your father? . . . I tell you what, Khalil! I want to go learn to be a teacher; perhaps your work may be to persuade our people that we want some new ways and much education!"

Khalil's eyes gleamed. "Yes, perhaps! I shall also want to learn more about machines, though, in between speeches . . . It may not be so very hard to persuade people, Selim. After all, it is now the law that all children, boys and girls, shall attend school until the age of twelve. Once we have the schools and the teachers—"

Katan interrupted, so greatly moved that she forgot her manners. "But thy father will never permit all this! Besides, it will not help Jasmin at all, for she is already more than twelve."

What a realistic child she was! Khalil regarded her with new interest. But before he could reply, a jeep rounded the turn, halted at the pine grove only a few yards away, and produced Major Schorr.

The major had visited Kfar Shalom a few times while Khalil had been staying there, but the two had been adroitly kept out of each other's sight. This time Khalil was blatantly, inescapably in view.

The major stood and stared at him with the expression of some one who has just found a scorpion in his shoe. Khalil did him one better. He looked at and through the officer as if he were a mere swarm of flies: a thing of Shaitan, but hardly worth noticing. Katan shrank back as if confronted by Shaitan in person, and Selim quite unconsciously completed the insult by gazing at the Yahudi with an expression of great compassion.

"Avram!" roared Schorr. "Avram! What in Tophet is this young *khutzpan* doing here?"

Instead of Avram, Malkah appeared. She had quite lost her usual calm. Her fists were on her hips, two flags of hot pink flew in her tanned cheeks, and her attitude lacked respect. "These happen to be friends of ours,

Major Schorr," she said, ice in her voice. "What's more, it's none of your business, anyhow! You're as much a visitor here as they are! Who do you military fellows think you are, anyway? This is a free country! Your job is to guard the borders, not interfere with our affairs!"

"I know what my job is, young lady, and I'm doing it!" he retorted when he found his voice. "I'm not as big a fool as you think. This boy was involved in that shooting you had here, and I think you know it as well as I do; and his whole village is up to the ears in plots and treason. He's probably spying on you this minute! Haven't you any better sense than to trust—"

"We've got better sense than to go around making enemies of people who only want to stay neutral!" returned Malkah doggedly. "And if you'd stop making trouble, perhaps we'd have some chance of making friends. Why don't you go play games on the Syrian border and leave us alone?" She jerked her brown head eastward rather pointedly, and glared.

Selim and Katan, who couldn't at all understand the rattle of angry Hebrew, nevertheless had a very good general idea of what was being said. Bismallah! What great warriors these Yahud women were! Khalil, who did manage to follow the conversation quite well, was slightly less astonished, for he was growing accustomed to Yahuda ways. But he had great difficulty not breaking into a cheer or at least a broad grin, which might not be altogether tactful under the circumstances—

and Khalil didn't want to make unnecessary trouble
... in fact, he had begun rather to fear for the safety of
the intrepid Malkah, and it was a relief when other
kibbutzniks began to appear, and then Avram showed
up.

"What is this, civil war?" he asked. His freckled face
was pleasant, but the major must somehow have found
it a trifle discouraging, for he didn't answer at once.
"Let's go inside and talk it over," suggested Avram,
and led the way inside.

"He winked at us!" whispered Katan reverently
when the whole group had vanished. "Or at least he
winked at Khalil. Didn't he?"

Khalil nodded, hiding his glow of pleasure at the
comradeship. "Why not?" he asked casually. "We're
friends, and none of us much like that other fellow." It
was nice to be on the same side as his chaverim here,
against another Yahudi. "I'd better get back to work.
The lathe isn't working right, and Yaacov asked me to
help him fix it." And he hurried off to the tool shed,
pleasantly conscious that Selim was much impressed
and Katan alight with admiration.

Avram found him when Major Schorr had gone,
blissfully immersed in wheels, wires, nuts and bolts,
and oil. He stood grinning. "I'd rather have your job
than mine," he remarked wryly.

Khalil grinned back. "Has he gone?"

"Yes, thank goodness!" Avram was at pains to make
no secret of his feelings. "He's like a terrier with a rat,

Khalil. He *knows* we've put something over on him.
Even has some crazy idea that you wanted to shoot him
or something." They grinned again, and then Avram
frowned. "All the same—Look, you'd better warn your
father when you go back, and keep your own eye open.
I've been wondering about Hassoun lately . . ."

He looked questioningly at Khalil, who nodded.
Hassoun had indeed been looking just a trifle too
pleased with something lately. And Khalil felt a strong
obligation to prevent any more trouble between his
village and the rest of Israel.

"Malkah has just told me that Moshe should be
completely fit again by next week," Avram said after a
moment. "I must tell you that all debts are ended, and
you may return home whenever you wish. Or after
Friday, anyway. We're having a party for you then, and
I don't think we can let you miss that."

Khalil, very much moved, looked quite wooden.
"You are sure I have made full recompense?" he demanded.

"To tell you the truth," replied Avram, "I rather
think we're in your debt now, Khalil. I hope you'll
give us the chance to repay. And—Khalil—You will
come back often? We'll miss you, chaver."

It would have surprised Moussa had he seen his son
and the Yahud mukhtar clasp hands like brothers.

Khalil lay awake again that night, torn between
wanting to go and wanting to stay. On one hand, it
would be good to return to the comfortable old ways,

to see his parents, to be once more the proud son of the mukhtar. On the other hand, life in Bab-il-Howa seemed suddenly without interest or merit. And he would miss the machinery—and the vigor and gaiety of the life here: the sociable evenings, the merry and muddled Hebrew-Arab language sessions, his new friends . . . Life was very complicated.

18. sedition in the village

Bab-il-Howa had grown much smaller, dirtier, smellier. The gutter down the twisting street stank, even though this was still the rainy season. Khalil stood in the doorway of his home, blinking into the dim interior, and suddenly felt himself to be an alien. He no longer fit into his own world—and he could never completely fit into the Yahud world, either. Brief anger spurted. This was Avram's doing! He had taken Khalil and changed him! . . . No, that wasn't fair. The anger was replaced by a sense of loss and dissatisfaction. Then his family rushed to welcome him, and he was being clasped in his mother's arms, and his father's.

"You are home with honor restored," pronounced Moussa with satisfaction. "Now all that is behind us. We are on good terms with Kfar Shalom, but each village can go its own way, neither interfering with the other. Wives, daughter, prepare a feast."

They at once turned to obey, bulky in their shapeless robes, submissive as servants. It was a very great shock after so long among the Yahud, and Khalil found himself smarting with resentment. His sister was at least the equal of any Yahuda at Kfar Shalom; nay better! Prettier, cleverer, with more spirit under the mask she was forced to wear. How unfair that she should never develop her gifts! How humiliating if other peoples should judge Arab women by appearances! He scowled.

Jasmin, though startled, scowled back wholeheartedly. She hadn't intended to annoy him; not yet, anyway. She had missed him terribly, and was overjoyed to see him again. But of course if he wanted to continue their old war without so much as an armistice in between, she didn't care. Just so long as he was here at all . . .

Khalil went on staring. For the first time he was seeing her not as his girl-twin, but simply as his twin: a being much like himself, with the same restless energy, the same need to do something and be something, the same impatience with keeping to old ways just because they were old. Why, she was his natural ally! They both needed to be freed and educated, and to help free others. And there was no time to lose.

"The school starts presently at Kafer Wadi," he observed obliquely, and saw Jasmin's head flip around so fast that her heavy braid swung. Anger and longing were vivid on her face.

Moussa pursed his lips disapprovingly, a trifle offended that the first school had not been started in his village—even though he had not been at all sure he wanted it. "Mahmoud teaches our boys all they need know," he said.

Khalil found himself possessed of a cunning that surprised him. He nodded. "That is true, oh my father. Ignorance is more pleasing to Allah than knowledge. Let our neighbors go learn things and send their children. All they want is to get rich and buy more land and build new houses. We are not so greedy."

Ahmed came out of his thoughts at the magic word "land" and looked deeply interested. Moussa frowned. He didn't think he cared for any of that speech, or for Khalil's tone of great authority, either. "When did thou become mukhtar of this village, oh second son?" he inquired acidly. "I am considering this matter of school, and when I have considered, I shall advise my people accordingly."

Khalil contrived to look slightly abashed. Had he actually fooled Father? Dared he go a bit further? He risked a glance at Jasmin's face and found it fixed on his with blank astonishment. He winked at her, producing a wave of delight that seemed almost to peal aloud. Alarmed, he frowned, and she managed to muffle it slightly—but it was still nearly as audible as a song. Was it possible that no one else heard it? Made bold, he pushed his luck a bit more.

"At least," he pronounced with an arrogance almost worthy of Yusif, "at least thou wilt not send girls to school. I know that for a certainty, and I told them so."

It was really a most appalling impudence. His family stared. A black haze of anger seemed to gather around Moussa's head. Zubaida held her breath, Hayat tried to become invisible, Kbeer Abou rumbled like a volcano. Only Jasmin sent Khalil a look of passionate gratitude and comprehension. All the love between them, diverted for so long, rushed forth at once.

"Thy stay with the Yahud has been very bad for thee," Moussa rumbled angrily. "Do you wish a beating?"

"Nay," protested Khalil, aggrieved. "I said nothing but what I knew you would say. I know you will never permit girls to go to school." And he looked unbearably smug.

Moussa had more than once used this kind of guile on others, but he had no defense against it himself, because it had never occurred to him that anyone would dare try it on him. Goaded, he fell into the trap.

"Then you are mistaken, impudent boy! I shall permit parents to send daughters if it is a good school and they see fit. Perhaps I shall even send the baby daughter when the time comes. I am considering the matter of sending Selim to the place where they train teachers, so that he may return and teach all of our children. Besides," he added prudently, "girls need go only for a year or two."

"But the law says until the age of twelve," objected Khalil, forgetting his guile. His father favored him with a dark look, edged with suspicion. His mother shot him a warning one. She knew what he was up to, for did she not sometimes use the same tactics herself? Did not all women, everywhere? But one must know when to stop, and now was the time.

Khalil swallowed the arguments on his tongue, and subsided. All the light had been momentarily extinguished from Jasmin's face with the new dashing of hope, and Khalil felt bitterly that he had failed her and himself. But then their eyes met and it was somehow all right again. What was the loss of a skirmish or two? They had hardly started their campaign . . .

"It is not that we are less than the Yahud!" proclaimed Khalil in a low but intense voice, letting his eyes sweep over his enthralled audience. It was a good idea to practice speech-making on his own family—or at least part of it. Ahmed and the women showed great interest and admiration, and they helped him to keep an eye on the door lest Father or Kbeer Abou should walk in.

"It is only that we have been doing nothing for many years, while they have been learning and doing many new things. Once it was we, the Arabs, who led the world in new things. Did you know," he went on, leaning forward, sparkling with new confidence and enthusiasm, "that it was *we* who invented numbers and mathematics, we who studied the stars, who gave medical knowledge to the West, we who built beautiful buildings, had great writers and poets, who were civi-

lized while the Western peoples were still savage barbarians? In truth, we are a very great people indeed,
only we have been asleep for a long time, and now we
must wake up and learn everything the Yahud know,
and more besides, and once again become the leaders
of the world."

Zubaida watched her son's face and nodded slowly to
herself. Allah had answered one of her prayers. Khalil
had stopped devouring himself and was out to reform
the world. Doubtless he would go to extremes at first,
but this was natural.

"Do not throw out all the old ways, my son," she
suggested. "It is the part of wisdom to see what is good,
and to keep it."

He paid little attention, of course. Later—

Jasmin had leaned forward, breathless. "And what
of me, oh my brother?" she whispered.

He nodded vigorously. It was true that just now he
was unable to see what could be done about Jasmin,
but inspiration would come. "Just go on talking to all
the other girls," he advised her. "I can tell thee more
things that I learned at Kfar Shalom. Make them all so
envious of Yahud girls that something will have to be
done for the sake of peace."

Jasmin looked martyred. She'd been doing that all
winter! "What sort of something?" she demanded.

"My friends at Kfar Shalom will help us get ideas,"
he temporized. "I shall go back every day, to learn
more about machines, and practice Hebrew, and—I

know, Jasmin!" His eyes gleamed with the daring of an idea. "You shall come visit, too! You will like the Yahud girls, and they can begin to teach you things. Surely you can find a little time when no one will miss you?"

He looked hopefully at Zubaida, who was torn between concern for Jasmin and dislike of deceiving her husband. Jasmin lowered her lashes as a veil over her eyes. "What a wonderful idea!" she sighed. "Please, Mother! Oh please!"

Zubaida consulted her intuition. Presently, reluctantly, she nodded. "If you will act with restraint and moderation," she decided, "and if you will do nothing against the law or the Koran . . ."

Ahmed said nothing. But he thought.

Thereafter a number of highly interesting conversations began to take place throughout the village. Khalil held the boys enthralled with his tales of Yahud machines and ways. Jasmin resumed her visits to Kfar Shalom—and this time with the approval and assistance of her mother and two brothers. Katan conscripted more little girls for reading lessons, and Selim spread insidious propaganda about the delights and advantages of education.

As for Zubaida, she astonished all of them, including herself. Gently, slowly, she began to drop small hints among the women. Did they know that Yahud women had a wonderful thing called soap, to make washing much easier and more effective? Nay, they even had machines to do the washing for them! Khalil had heard about them at the Yahud village, which did not yet have one themselves, but would do so just as soon as a thing called electricity was put there . . .

What a pity it was that Yemna's eyes gave so much trouble with the sewing! Yahud women had a machine that could sew more quickly than ten women! There was one in the Kfar Shalom now, in fact, for it did not even need the thing called electricity . . .

Yahud women did not need to grind meal by hand. They had very many clever and useful things to make work easier. And with the extra time, they did interesting things. Nay, even their Arab sisters in many villages had these things. And there were classes and meetings that they attended, where they learned better ways of caring for families and tending illness, and even learned such things as reading and arithmetic if they liked . . .

"This is wicked talk!" spat Basna one day. "I think thy son had an evil spell put on him at that Yahud village, and has put it on thee. I shall tell my husband the things you are saying, and he shall tell *thy* husband. Moreover, Allah will punish thee—as he punishes me, though I am a good woman," she added, her anger crumpling into misery.

"Thy baby is worse?" exclaimed Zubaida compassionately. "Oh, Basna, if only—No. If it were my baby, I would take him to the nurse at Kfar Shalom, who is very skilled at curing people, Khalil says. But then I do not have thy strength of mind."

Basna snorted and stalked home. But that afternoon she took a dirty swaddled bundle over the ridge to the Yahud village. And although the baby's recovery was doubtless due to Allah's will and had nothing to do with the Yahuda, Basna stopped opposing Zubaida's propaganda.

Jasmin listened to her mother with new respect. Bismallah! What a very paragon of wisdom and guile! Jasmin's own accomplishments seemed almost petty by comparison, for the young were less conservative and more open to new ideas. Jasmin could go further than Zubaida in subversion.

Why, she demanded, should girls not have equal education with boys? Why should women not have equal rights with men? Why should they not choose their own husbands? Yahud women had all these rights —and look how Allah caused the Yahud to prosper!

This last point was particularly effective. "He even caused them to win the war!" Amira recalled in awe. "Mashallah!"

"*Allah ysallmak!*" chorused the others reverently.

"Pooh!" said Nejmi, refusing to be impressed. "I don't believe it. It was Shaitan who helped them. Besides," she added, wavering, "how could we have all those things?"

"Why not?" returned Jasmin. "Are we not learning to read? Moreover, I am learning to speak Hebrew, as well. Khalil is teaching me," she bragged. "He is very pleased with me. He says I learn almost as quickly as a boy and more quickly than many."

"Will you teach me?" demanded Amira at once. "Please, Jasmin! I want to be an educated female, too!"

"And I!" breathed Shuhda. "But don't tell my father!"

Jasmin made a wry face. "Do you think I'm crazy? What of *my* father?"

"Just as I thought," announced Nejmi, tossing a pious head. "You are deceiving your father, wicked girl! Someone ought to tell him!"

Jasmin shot her a ferocious glance. "If anyone does," she announced, "she'll get a worse beating for listening than I for talking, because her parents are stricter than mine. And," she added ominously, "she might get another one for being a telltale."

Nejmi, silenced by this threat, sulked for a while, and then decided that since she was already incriminated she might as well go the whole way. Thereafter, had anyone bothered to notice, the percussive sounds of Hebrew could be heard now and then in girlish mutterings.

But nobody noticed. The women were engrossed in the food for thought that Zubaida was doling out to them in tantalizing tidbits. The men never heeded female chatter, and in any case, they too had other matters to think about. A small, hard nucleus still centered around Jawad's brothers and brothers-in-law, and Hassoun's followers. The others found themselves intrigued by tales of Yahud cars and houses and tractors, of light or water at a flick of the wrist, of talking over wires, and other modern magic—all, it was said, being used by a great many of their Arab brethren in Israel. And if other Arabs could have these things . . .

And so the currents moved and gathered force as winter passed. And Moussa said nothing.

19. the explosion

It was February, the one-eyed month, with warm sun and showers alternating, and a sudden urgency of growing things. And in Moussa's household tenseness slowly turned to bewilderment. For it was impossible that he had not noticed something of the talk and ideas surging through the village! And yet what he did was —precisely nothing.

They should not have been surprised. Moussa was not an impulsive man. He had noticed, but he was not really doing nothing: he was thinking about it. Better to wait than to do the wrong thing; moreover, perhaps there was no need to do anything. It was natural that there should be unrest just now; did he not feel it himself? It would no doubt pass, and all would be as it was. Even Hassoun and his fire-eating friends would presently tire of their plotting, and with Jawad gone there was little danger of their doing more than talk. And so he waited.

And then one day Alouf passed by the spot where Katan and her young friends were having a writing class. Alouf, who kept forgetting that a big boy nearly grown should not be interested in the doings of small females, paused. Katan had drawn a shape in the soft earth with a stick, and the others were copying it. The shape reminded Alouf vaguely of the days in Mahmoud's school, when he had tried vainly to learn to read. He came closer, staring.

"What are you doing?" he asked.

The little girls flushed, hung their heads, and burst into shrill giggles. Only Katan brazened it out. "Oh, we are just playing," she said, casually wiping out the letter.

Alouf quite failed to see anything odd about their behavior, but he was interested. He twisted his head to look at one of the other marks in the earth. "It looks like writing," he pointed out.

"Oooh!" squealed Katan above renewed giggling. "How could girls write? We're just drawing things, Alouf!"

"Oh," said Alouf, and went his way satisfied. But because it was the most interesting thing he had seen that day, he mentioned it to some of the men in the coffeehouse.

"Eh?" demanded Kbeer Abou, cocking an ear. "What was that?"

Most of the men paid no attention, knowing and caring little about children's games. Kassem and Amira's father knew of the reading and rather approved. They exchanged glances.

"Nothing of importance," said Kassem hastily.

But Alouf, pleased to have found an interested audience, bawled his story into Kbeer Abou's ear . . .

Moussa and Mahmoud were having their running game of chess at the small table in the courtyard. They sucked peacefully at water pipes, one eye on Yusif, who was teasing the goat tethered to the olive tree. Mahmoud looked at his host and friend with affection and amusement as he studied the board. He had heard that in some places men lived peacefully on the slopes of smoking mountains, and were invariably surprised and indignant when the mountain sooner or later exploded into flame . . .

Moussa moved a pawn. Mahmoud considered it. All things would come to fruit in Allah's own time. Most of them were no direct concern of his unless Moussa chose to consult him. But there was one matter—

He took the pawn. "Thy son Yusif has a good mind," he observed. Moussa grunted noncommittally. "He is not as clever as Khalil," Mahmoud went on, "but he should be a leader of our people in this new nation. Unfortunately, I think he will not."

Yusif, about to poke the goat with a sharp stick to see what he would do, looked up, startled and displeased. Moussa raised his thick eyebrows and his gaze. "And why is this, oh imam?"

Mahmoud sucked on his pipe. "Education will be necessary among his generation. And how can he learn, oh Moussa, when he does not attend school more than one day in three?"

"YUSIF!" roared Moussa.

Yusif had already begun a swift, furtive movement around the olive tree. He halted, meditating flight. He decided against it, mostly because his father was between him and the gate.

"Come here!" commanded Moussa.

Yusif took a deep breath and strutted over, chin high. He was not going to like this interview, but if he couldn't avoid it, he'd meet it half way. His black eyes were not quite impudent.

"Is this true?" demanded his father.

Yusif met the fierce gaze fearlessly. "I do not need to go to school. Already I know more than I need."

"You know far less than the other boys," Mahmoud corrected him. "And the son of the mukhtar should know more. Furthermore, you set a bad example."

"Where do you go when not at school?" asked Moussa.

Yusif looked at him speculatively, and decided it would do no good to lie, but merely earn him an extra hard beating. "To the Yahud village," he said defiantly.

Moussa stared. "What for?" he demanded, incredulous.

"I go to visit my good friend Leo. He is a very great hero, and he admires me very much, even though he speaks Arabic badly. I learn things from him that

Mahmoud does not teach me," he added craftily. "I shall soon be cleverer than anyone in Bab-il-Howa."

Moussa was silent, gathering thunderclouds. Mahmoud spoke mildly. "It is good to learn more things than I can teach. But it is not good to learn them instead of what I teach. If you wish to be a noble and admired man, you must learn the Koran, and if you wish to know very much about anything whatever, you must be able to read well."

"I can read very well!" bragged Yusif indignantly. "You said so!"

"I said you had improved lately," corrected his teacher. "That is something altogether different. You are still a very bad reader." A twinkle crept into the deep-set eyes, nearly hidden by the massed wrinkles of his eyelids. "I believe a little girl could do better."

Jasmin, arriving with a tray of coffee and pita, nearly dropped it. Yusif spluttered. But the old man had no intention of telling about Katan; he merely smiled at them benignly.

Moussa, having now collected his wrath about him and got it in order, now spoke, his lower lip jutting outward from his beard. "All this," he said, "is of lesser importance than thy deceit, my son. Did you ask my permission for such visits? No. You knew I would not approve. You shall have a severe beating, and you will never go there again. We are friends with those Yahud, but we do not mix with them."

Yusif's small round face became an alarming shade

of red, and his fists clenched. Jasmin stood like a stone, still holding the tray, catching her breath. Yusif had no sense of loyalty, much less of noble self-sacrifice; he was not at all the sort to suffer alone if he could help it. Therefore Jasmin feared the worst—and she was not mistaken.

"Why shouldn't I go?" yelled Yusif, his small body quite rigid with rage. "Everyone else goes! Khalil goes, and Selim goes, and even Jasmin and Katan go!"

"I do not believe thee," rumbled Moussa, but belief had begun to close around his mind even as Yusif spoke. And it was at this moment that Kbeer Abou arrived, squealing and sputtering, to pour out the tale of little girls learning to read and write.

For once he had his son-in-law's full attention. Moussa swelled with wrath. His eye fell balefully on the spot where Jasmin had vanished to give warning, leaving her tray on the ground. Even now three veiled heads peered fearfully from behind the grape arbor, wondering where and when the lightning would strike first.

Kbeer Abou, encouraged, ranted on and on. Moussa, having got the information from amid the invective, had stopped listening and was consulting with himself. Not for the first time he wondered whether it might be Shaitan who wagged Kbeer Abou's tongue. Shaitan, in fact, had almost certainly been active among his own family, and even, it would seem, throughout his village. Moussa could hardly believe that this sort of thing had been going on all winter behind his back! Was he mukhtar or was he not?

He put the question tartly when he had gathered the villagers together. They, having heard it before, agreed mildly that he was mukhtar. But they did not all seem quite as abashed or as pacific as they might. Instead, there was a certain amount of acrid discussion. Some of the men said that they liked their little daughters to learn to read, and some of the women hinted that they would like to have modern magic machines to wash clothing, like their cousins in Nazareth. (Someone else muttered that Moussa was a Yahudi-lover and a traitor to his own people, but the owner of that voice was careful that it only added to the general atmosphere and was not heard by the mukhtar.)

Moussa regarded them with thunderous displeasure. This was insurrection! His own sister Yemna talking to him about machines! Even Basna, that stronghold of conservatism, was shouting about nurses and clinics for sick babies.

"Bismallah!" he roared at last. "Corruption and evil have come to Bab-il-Howa! What is wrong with you all? Our ways are old and honorable. Any who do not like them need not stay in this village! I have spoken!" And he turned into his house to attend to his erring family.

It was a painful evening for everyone but the triumphant Kbeer Abou. Silence hung thick and black, subduing even Yusif, reducing Hayat to silent tears. The storm had not yet broken, for Moussa was still considering what was best to do. Moreover, he was waiting to get over the peak of his anger, lest he be unjust.

His anger was taking a long time to die down. His children had deceived him, flouted his authority, and, he strongly suspected, it was they who had aroused the discontent in the village. Even Zubaida seemed to be exchanging glances with the twins that were not merely sympathetic but downright conspiratorial! It was quite unsupportable! Was there no loyalty? At least he could thank Allah for his sweet young Hayat and his good, steady, reliable eldest son . . .

And then Ahmed looked up from his wooden plow. "Yahud machines make better crops. I have seen."

He went on calmly splicing the wooden handle, not glancing up, while his words seemed to echo in a vast silence. "They have said we may use them," he added presently.

"Bismallah!" breathed his father. "Thou too? Surely Shaitan is loose in my village!"

Ahmed thought it over. "Shaitan doesn't like good crops," he decided at last. "Machines and fertilizer and other Yahud things improve crops, so they can't be of Shaitan."

Forsaken even by Ahmed, Moussa appealed to reason and tradition. "Have we not always lived thus? Have we not been contented? Would you now forsake our old ways and have ugly, noisy monsters to offend our eyes and ears?"

Ahmed nodded single-mindedly. It was Khalil who felt a pang for the old, peaceful ways, already doomed. Perhaps after all it would be better not to change too many things too quickly . . .

"You see?" shrilled Kbeer Abou triumphantly. "You see? I told thee! Evil and corruption they bring! All thy family is corrupted save only me and my grandson, who only visited the Yahud village in order to spy out their weaknesses. Come to my side, Yusif. Thou and I know the truth. We shall go out together and destroy them all!"

Yusif stood on one leg and rubbed a dirty foot across his ankle. He liked being in favor with Grandfather, who spoiled him and who told exciting tales—but Yusif was no longer interested in destroying the Yahud, who were now friends of his. With a cheeky glance from the corners of his eyes at Kbeer Abou, he strutted over and took what he felt was a heroic stance between Ahmed and the twins.

It was unmistakably a united front. Even Khalil and Jasmin, after warring for most of their lives, were now as one. Even Zubaida was clearly seriously torn between loyalty and conviction. Even Hayat—? Moussa looked at her. She looked at the cradle where her baby slept, and then back at him.

"Yahud babies do not often sicken and die," she whispered with drooped head and downcast eyes. "They have ways to keep them healthy."

It was the final defiance. Moussa rose in terrifying silence and strode out into the night.

He left behind him a silence charged with assorted emotions, none of them very pleasant. Kbeer Abou started to give them all a piece of his mind, but he found that they were all staring at him with a fixed hostility that was altogether disconcerting. He decided to beat them all soundly another day, and hobbled out to the coffeehouse rather hurriedly.

When he had gone, the twins turned on Yusif. "Sneak!" hissed Jasmin. "Viper! Tattletale! Coward! Horrible little scorpion!" She was very near tears. Never to see Chava and the others again! Never to have any more hope of anything . . . "Mean, leprous, wicked, changeling of demons!" she squalled so threateningly that Yusif took refuge behind Hayat, from where he made rude faces at Jasmin. He didn't in the least understand why she was so upset. Surely anyone would have tattled in order to divert Father's wrath?

Jasmin seriously considered dragging him out and wringing his neck. She glanced at Khalil, who was in complete accord. United, they started forward. Yusif wailed aloud. Life was clearly going to be very trying for a while.

"Leave Yusif to me," commanded Zubaida, not at all brightening that young man's future. Zubaida, if possible, was even more alarming than the twins. "The question now is what will thy father do? We cannot defy him or disobey him, oh my children."

Jasmin's anger departed and despair closed around her. The future stretched gray and bleak as a prison sentence. Her lip trembled, enormous tears poured silently down the fawn satin of her cheeks into the flour she had been grinding. Khalil, nearly as depressed, put an awkward hand on her shoulder.

Gloom filled the house. Ahmed looked with hatred at the wooden plow. Hayat stared at the cradle as if seeing ranks of plague-demons waiting to kill her baby without Yahud medicine. Zubaida looked at them with grief and at her twins with fear. Fiery by nature, intense and impatient, a little drunk now with the strength of their new unity—they were only a step from open rebellion. Allah prevent it! There was too much family love; they and Moussa could hurt one another too badly! She bent to her work, troubled.

Then Yusif, never quenched for long, popped his hard round head out from behind Hayat, and scampered over to the smouldering twins, having totally forgotten the recent unpleasantness.

"Never mind," he whispered. "When Father is deposed, one of us will be mukhtar, and we shall do as we like."

"Little weasel!" Khalil turned a snubbing shoulder. But Jasmin, more familiar with the workings of Yusif's mind, quickened to attention.

"What do you mean, when Father is deposed?" she taunted in tones perfectly calculated to bring forth everything he knew.

"It is true!" he asserted, indignant. "I heard it myself, and more than once. They are very cross at Father, and—"

"Who are?" Khalil was now gratifyingly interested.

Yusif expanded even more freely. "Oh, Hassoun, and some of his friends, and Jawad, and—"

"Little liar! Jawad is exiled over the border!"

"I am a very great liar when I wish to be." Yusif looked smug. "But this time I am telling the truth. One night Jawad came back, and he was in Hassoun's house. I heard his voice, so I looked in and saw him, and then I listened. He had some other Syrians with him, and they said Father was a Yahudi-lover, which is a very silly thing to say when he is so very much *not* a Yahudi-lover, and I almost told them so at once; but then I thought they might be unreasonable if they knew I was listening, and besides I wanted to hear more, so I didn't."

It had a most ominous ring of truth. Yusif's imaginings were never anything like this. Jasmin and Khalil looked at each other in growing alarm, and then over their shoulders at the women and Ahmed who had returned to their various tasks.

"And what else did you hear, oh clever spy?" asked Khalil.

"Oh, they said Yahudi-lovers shouldn't be mukhtars, and must be punished, and perhaps they would shoot him or blow him up, and have Grandfather mukhtar instead; and then they talked of having another war with the Yahud and exterminating them all and taking the land, but this time I think I shall be on the side of the Yahud, and between Leo and me, we shall win even more easily than before."

Somehow he seemed to have lost his audience. The twins were looking at each other with growing terror. The main kernel of the story sounded all too likely! And where was Father now? Out in the hills, without a doubt, where he always walked when he was disturbed or wished to think. And after what had happened today . . . Was it already too late? Might he be lying somewhere now, dead or wounded?

Khalil half rose on his knees. "Ahmed and I could —" But Jasmin shook her head, and he saw it, too. Out on the hills in the dark— It was hopeless. There was little chance of finding him, and if they did, it might be only to call attention to him for any assassin who might be around. No, all they could do tonight was pray. As soon as Father returned, if he returned, they would of course warn him.

"Hassoun is a big talker," Khalil told Jasmin reassuringly, "but he never does anything. Or at least," he added, remembering one or two incidents, "not very often. It will be all right; you'll see."

Jasmin nodded, half reassured. All the same, the night crept on and on, and he did not come. They went to bed, and she lay awake on her small pallet next to Mother, listening to the breathing inside and the wind around the house. Kbeer Abou, over on the men's side of the room, snored so loudly and with such a revolting variety of noises that he was almost as disagreeable asleep as awake. She stiffened. Did she hear the rattle of far-off gunfire? Not Father! Please Allah, keep him safe!

But if it was gunfire, it went on for too long to be an ambush. No doubt it was just an ordinary border raid or skirmish. Jasmin began to relax, and then was wide awake again as the outer gate creaked. He was back!

The minutes passed, and he did not come in. She must have imagined the gate . . . But surely there were other sounds around the house? In a lull of the wind she heard the hiss of someone convinced that loud whispers were inaudible to anyone not supposed to hear. Then another thump.

Jasmin could bear it no longer. Slipping off her mat, she crawled over to Khalil and poked him awake. It wasn't difficult, for he was only half dozing, uneasy despite his own encouraging words. He became wide awake instantly. "What is it? Is Father home?"

She put a small hard hand to his mouth and her mouth to his ear. "No. Come and listen. I think someone is outside."

He rolled off his mat at once, ears alert. Only wind —and then a small grating noise against the house itself, over in Father's corner. It didn't sound like rats. Was it inside or out? They crept across the room, to the dark and silent corner where Father should have been sleeping but was not.

And then the world flew to pieces in a roar of orange and yellow, a chorus of yells, a rumble of stones.

Stunned and blinded, the twins crouched where they had fallen. Then a sense of compelling urgency made Khalil open his eyes just as the whole corner of the stone house began to collapse. There was no time to get out of the way, no time to haul Jasmin to safety; only time to give one despairing shout and hurl her backwards, his own body over hers.

20. out of the dark

When he left the house, Moussa stood at the top of the
street for a few moments, the wind whipping his tob,
and the pointed corners of his khaffiya lashing his face.
He didn't notice, for he was staring down at the dark
shape of his village, crouched against the hill in the
dusk, a faint flicker of light here and there from narrow windows. This was his village, his responsibility,
his people; and they now defied his authority!

A shadow flickered across the narrow space between
two houses, and a scuffling sound reminded him briefly
and uneasily of other rustlings by night these last
months. But this was only rats foraging in the gutter.
In any case, it was not now the Yahudi-haters who
troubled him.

He strode out past the houses, into the vast peace of
the hills, and presently stood still, massive and solid as
a bit of the land, staring unseeing down into the dark
bowl of the valley. He no longer felt quite as sure of his
own rightness. Phrases fragmented against his mind.
"Would you snatch food from their mouths?" . . . "Do

you forbid Allah the right to permit change?" . . . "Machines make better crops." Was it possible that he was wrong? Did Allah indeed wish His people to change in a changing world?

But even if this was true, how far was it true? How much change? Surely not ugly sights and noises; not beauty and peace sacrificed for speed and efficiency; not humanity enslaved and harassed by the tyranny of its own progress! Never! New ways, he conceded grudgingly, doubtless gave comfort of body, but the old ways gave peace of mind.

Was there no compromise, no way to have the one without destroying the other? What did Allah want, that he had given this land unto the Yahud? Alone in the wind, Moussa prayed for guidance to His will. Then, the sharp edges of his vexation eased, he walked slowly on across the sloping fields, to the threshing place.

From here he could look down upon Kfar Shalom, the bright flicker of lamps gleaming in narrow slits around shuttered windows. No sound could be heard because of distance and wind, but the feel of the place was one of industry and cheer. Had they found such a compromise? They were good, these young people, even though they had an air of rather brash self-confidence at times that Moussa found irritating.

They would lend machines, Ahmed had said! How condescending! They would confer favors! No no! Wrong to accept such paternalism; disastrous to plunge his people headlong into Western ways!

A small compromise perhaps. Water in pipes some day, and a school which even girls might attend for a year or two. Let Selim go learn to be a teacher, that there be no need for one from the outside. Let the women and Ahmed learn one or two new ideas to make housework more efficient and improve crops—but no machines. As for Khalil—

On the crest of the hill, high to the north, black shapes moved for an instant against a slaty sky. They had not the look of a border patrol, being too furtive, and too robe-shaped. And if they weren't patrol, they must be infiltrators—either harmless Arabs trying to rejoin their families or a different sort bent on mischief.

Moussa's frown darkened slowly into burning anger against all men of hate and violence, men who invaded a peaceful country, attacked its citizens, interfered with the pattern of life. Moreover, these enemy marauders were to blame for the galling restrictions laid upon Israeli Arabs, who must always be under suspicion of helping them.

Moussa pondered. What had those shapes in mind? Whatever they did might cause the suspicious Major Schorr to blame his village. And what if they should attack Kfar Shalom, who were well-meaning and likeable? Moussa suddenly discovered that he was really quite fond of Avram and his young people, and wanted no harm to come to them. And he found himself already striding down the hill. A word of warning would do no one any harm . . .

Before he reached the pine grove, there was a sound of voices, and the round yellow eyes of flashlights coming toward him. In a moment he found himself uncomfortably illumined by one of them, while ominous sounds from the surrounding blackness told of a rifle in readiness. Then the light quickly dropped away and shone politely instead on the apologetic and relieved face of the red-headed Moshe.

"Oh, it's you!" he exclaimed. "Il hamdillah! Allah's hand must be in this, for we were just coming to visit thee, oh Mukhtar, and to ask thy help."

When Moussa answered, his voice was both puzzled and ironic. "Indeed? But what could the Yahud, who can do everything, want with my help?"

Moshe, at times inclined to be prickly, frowned and was poked by the more perceptive and tactful Chaim.

"I regret if we have ever given thee that impression, oh Mukhtar. We are not so foolishly conceited. It is true that we have certain kinds of knowledge—but we are aware that you have great wisdom, which is not at all the same thing, and which is surely even more important."

Moussa was at once mollified. Perhaps the Yahud were not as cocky as he had thought. A touch of humility was becoming in the young.

"What is it that I may do for thee?" he asked benignly.

"Our very best cow lies ill," Moshe explained. "We don't know what to do. Khalil has told us that you have a healing magic with sick animals. Will you come?"

Moussa's hesitation was only a pretense. He would never have refused his help to a suffering creature, had it belonged to his worst enemy. Still, a certain form must be maintained. "Have you not a healing-woman among you?"

"We have no animal-doctor at this kibbutz," explained Chaim. "Only a people-nurse, and she doesn't know what is wrong. We need thy wisdom, Mukhtar, for our knowledge is not enough."

Moussa inclined his head with the graciousness of a king. Much was now changed. There was no longer a modern people conferring favors upon a lesser one, but two villages, each able to help the other. It was gratifying to have the Yahud recognize this and ask for his help. No doubt there would be other matters in which he could benefit them. In fact, there was one at hand now.

"Come," he said, leading the way briskly toward the kibbutz. "I shall help thy cow if I can. But I came this way in order to give thy mukhtar Avram a warning to keep careful watch this night, for I have seen figures on the hilltop that do not belong there. Where is thy cow?"

The night was very old when he finally raised his head from the sick cow and met the anxious eyes of Avram. "It will be well with her now," he said wearily.

Avram looked at him with admiration. "Khalil was right about thy healing power," he said. "I think no animal-doctor could have saved her."

"That is true," said Moussa simply and without vanity. Between him and Avram there passed a look of mutual reverence for this gift from God.

"Come and have coffee and food," said Avram. "Will thy family be worried? I should have sent some-one to—"

The rest was shattered by an eruption of shots and yells an uncomfortably short distance away. "The visitors you predicted!" said Avram. His voice was calm, but he had seized his rifle from against the wall and was out of the shed as he spoke.

Moussa followed, dazed for the moment by surprise and noise. A full moon had risen, so that he could see figures moving above, at the edge of the young orchard. The other kibbutzniks were pouring from the dormitories, some clad in sleeping garments, all with rifles and an air of businesslike and calm efficiency. Moussa found a moment to marvel. He had never realized that these Yahud—hardly more than children— must sleep with their guns, live in expectation of attack! And how bold and cool they were in the face of danger! Moussa felt proud of them.

There was an explosion much too near to be pleasant. Another, and one end of a dormitory flew into splinters. A third—and the small shed was a heap of rubble from which there came one dying moo. The cow would never recover, after all . . . and implacable hatred crystallized in Moussa.

A girl running toward the battle line fell suddenly.

Voices called for Malkah, and the nurse and another girl were there in a moment to carry her off on a stretcher. Moussa strode over and picked up the fallen rifle. Then he walked on, on to the line of battle, where he found Avram and moved into position beside him.

Avram made room as naturally as if they had been brothers. The attack was already collapsing. It had been a clever and vicious one, far better organized than most such raids. Had it not been for Moussa's warning and the extra guard, Kfar Shalom might indeed have been wiped out. But the efficiency of the defense was causing a decided loss of enthusiasm among the attackers, and when a huge robed and bearded figure suddenly loomed in the moonlight amid the Yahud roaring *"Allaho akbar!"*, they lost all heart and went home. Clearly Allah was in a bad humor that night.

It was over. Some of the attackers lay where they had fallen. The others fled back up the hill, pursued by angry kibbutzniks. Avram quickly organized the remainder, some to stay on guard, some to help care for wounded, some to assess the damage. Moussa remained at Avram's side, aiding where he could, quite identifying himself with these gallant young people.

One girl, Leah, was dead. Four others had slight wounds. The cow and several other animals had been killed, and Moussa tended two injured ones. One end of the girl's dormitory was a wreck, the barn was damaged, but the telephone lines had not been cut; and

Avram at once phoned the nearest army center for re-inforcements and medical help. He reported concisely what had happened, and then Moussa saw his face darken with sudden anger.

"They did not!" he snapped. "Tophet, Major; the mukhtar stood beside me and helped fight them off! If it hadn't been for his warning—Never mind, I'll talk to you later; I haven't got time now!"

He slammed down the receiver and met Moussa's twinkling eye ruefully. The mukhtar didn't under-stand Hebrew, but he had a splendidly accurate idea of what had been said, all the same. The situation was not without humor. Arab and Yahudi together against first Arab, and then Yahudi . . . But it was not the time to be amused.

"I have seen to the injured animals," he announced as if he owned the place.

"Thank you, chaver," said Avram gratefully, turn-ing to the half-dozen kibbutzniks who waited to give their reports. "But don't neglect thy own village. If they have heard the shooting—"

"No," said Moussa. "The wind blows from there to here, with much sound of its own, and the shoulder of the hill rises between. If it were the other way around—"

And as if a malignant god had been listening, the sound of explosion came muffled but clear from Bab-il-Howa.

21. dawn

Khalil rose slowly from a place of dark currents that whirled him downward, small and lost, to the accompaniment of a whining, buzzing sound that he found most unpleasant. But things seemed even more unpleasant out of the place. Something was on his legs, and it hurt. There was an astonishing tumult of shouting and wailing, and when he opened his eyes, there was a patch of most irrational moonlight shining across him. Ridiculous. How could moonlight get inside the house?

Memory swept back, and he realized that he was lying across something soft and motionless. Jasmin! Urgently Khalil raised his shoulders. She lay utterly still, her face pearl in the moonlight, the heavy curve of her lashes unmoving on her cheeks.

"Jasmin!" he cried, and saw that his mother knelt beside them, feeling for a heartbeat in the thin young throat or chest. Zubaida's calm was a frail wall holding back terror and grief, doubled by the unaccountable absence of Moussa.

Khalil's consciousness spread a little. There was movement near him, where Ahmed was frantically working at the pile of stones and rubble pinning the twins down, and harshly—Ahmed harsh!—commanding the sobbing Hayat and Yusif and the screeching Kbeer Abou to help. Then Mother's voice, ragged as that barbed wire on the hilltop, informing the old man that if he did not shut his mouth at once, she would personally stuff it with his own louse-filled beard. The screeching turned into stupefied silence, and Zubaida turned back to her injured children. Khalil closed his eyes again, for the pain in his legs was very bad. But through the roaring sound of his head, and another outside in the courtyard, he could now hear the voices of Selim and his father helping Ahmed.

And then Kassem's alarmed cry. "Stop! Wait! If we move any more, the rest of the wall will fall on them!"

Khalil no longer cared very much.

Outside in the courtyard, other unpleasant things were going on. Most of the village men were gathered there, brought by this attack to a single frame of mind. Vengeance was necessary—and here were the culprits. To be sure, Hassoun was already dead, slain by the blast. But here were Jawad and three Syrians, either injured or caught trying to run away. They knew what to expect, for the Arab code of retribution is strong, but neither swift nor merciful, as Jawad himself had helped demonstrate often. The whining,

groveling Jawad considered Hassoun to be the lucky
one . . .

But he was, after all, lucky as well. The headlights of
a Yahud truck began to zigzag up the hill, and the
Yahud might easily wish to turn the whole matter over
to the Law, which would be highly unsatisfactory.
Long knives flickered in the moonlight and vanished
again under robes.

The headlights roused Khalil again as they stabbed
through the open door and lighted the jagged hole in
the wall. He now felt that there were two of him, one
watching with detached clarity while the other sank
again into swirling darkness. The pain in his legs had
risen from red to vivid orange, and was now changing
to smoky yellow. The pressure was even worse than the
pain, and when he heard Moussa's voice and saw the
bulk of his shape, he heard himself cry out. "Father!"

Father was there, infinitely strong and comforting,
his big hands gentle upon his children. "It's Jasmin!"
Khalil whispered. "I think she's dead."

"No," said Malkah, miraculously there as well.
Khalil didn't know until much later that she had left
her wounded chaverim in order to come. In his dazed
state he couldn't at all understand her being there.
And surely that was Avram and Leo and some others
climbing on the rubble, risking their own lives in
order to topple the dangerous bit of wall outward?
Now many hands tore at the stones, and presently
there was the infinite relief of the pressure vanishing

from his legs, followed at once by greater pain, and Malkah saying they were broken but not too badly, and then the prick of a needle in his arm.

After that it all became a dream in which he fought sleepiness just long enough to see Jasmin freed as well, to see Malkah examine her with a grave face, and then turn to Moussa.

"Someone has already gone down the road to meet the doctor and to bring him here instead of to Kfar Shalom. But she needs more than a doctor: she needs you. Keep her alive, Moussa! Only you can do it!"

Then, for everyone in the ruined stone house, seconds and minutes spun themselves into meaningless threads of time. Moussa held the limp hands of his daughter in his own and worked as he had never worked before.

"Jasmin, little one," he called, not caring at all who heard. "Little flower, child of spirit, near to my heart! Do not die, small daughter. Come back. Listen to me. Thou shalt live. Thou shalt go to a Yahud hospital, where they will make thee well again. Thou shalt have thy heart's desire and learn to read like any boy. Tell her, Avram! They shall teach her in the hospital if I command it. Do you hear that, daughter? Moreover—" He recklessly abandoned principles in all directions. "Moreover, thou shalt marry whom thy heart desires when the time comes. Live, little daughter! Live, for I love thee, and the moon would leave the sky if I lost thee."

There was a world of melted rainbow where one floated in radiance and joy. Jasmin felt herself being tugged away from it, very much against her will. But the thing that tugged her seemed to be a shaft of love and tenderness, like sunlight shining upwards, and she slid down upon it until she could see Father's house, all ruined and torn open at one end, and groups of silent people—and Khalil and herself lying still. How odd to see herself! She must be hurt, for Father was kneeling at her side and talking to her. Or at least he was talking to her body, perhaps not understanding that she was quite out of it and up here somewhere. She rather liked being out of it. It felt like Arabian Nights, free and happy; and she had an idea that if she were to go back down there and get inside, her body would close around her again like a prison, and prove to be extremely uncomfortable. On the whole, she thought, she would rather not.

But Father kept calling. And then, somehow, Khalil seemed to be partly out of his body, too, and urging her to return. Jasmin drifted nearer, found herself listening to Father's words as well as feeling the love in them—and then she found that she had got into her body again without really knowing it. Pain began closing in, but when she opened her eyes and saw Father's face, she couldn't really be sorry. She hadn't wanted to leave her family, after all, in spite of the rainbow radiance. That would be there later, when her body was old and not much use, and she didn't want it any more.

It was quite a nice body now, even though it seemed to be rather smashed up at the moment. But Malkah and the Yahud hospital would fix that; Father had just promised—hadn't he?

She took a deep breath, even though it hurt badly. There was a circle of faces above her, lit by one of the bright Yahud lamps, and all the faces took deep breaths as well. Tears began rolling down Mother's lined cheeks, and Malkah put her fingers on Jasmin's wrist, and everyone seemed waiting for her to do or say something remarkable.

She looked up at Father, whose love was still holding her here, firmly attached to earth. Had he really said the things she thought she had heard? Best to make sure here and now.

"Learn things?" she demanded in what turned out to be the faintest of whispers.

He nodded, gripping her hand more tightly. "I have promised."

"Khalil too?" persisted Jasmin. "And Katan? And Amira?" This was her moment: the moment when she was the dearest thing in Father's universe, when he could deny her nothing. Jasmin loved him for caring so much—but it would be very silly indeed to waste an opportunity which might never come again, and she milked it mercilessly. "May we all go to visit Kfar Shalom? Whenever we like?" she went on, her voice still a weak whisper, but carrying such strength of determination that they all stared and Malkah began to hope, after all.

"Bismallah!" said Moussa, blinking down at his daughter, who suddenly reminded him very strongly of someone. Was it himself? He found himself nodding to all her demands, which amounted to nothing short of blackmail. She'd live if he made it worth her while . . . Little devil!

"Ye may visit so long as ye are obedient and well-behaved children," he amended sternly, for it would not do to diminish his authority.

By the time the doctor arrived, no one had any serious doubt that Jasmin would live. She had entirely too firm a grip on the advantages she had seized to consider giving them up now. It was true that she lost consciousness when they moved her with infinite care to a stretcher, but only for a moment. She made herself come back yet again to the blurred world, graying to the east, where the Yahud doctor talked to Father and Khalil lay in another stretcher next to her. It was as if their hands met, though it was only their eyes—sleepy with drugs, wide with pain and wonder and apprehension. Things seemed overwhelming now, and unreal, and rather out of hand. Where were they being taken? Surely, Father and Mother were coming too?

But this was not at all certain. Moussa had his responsibility to his village, which was in an uproar. Moreover, there would be official inquiries about the events of the night, and they were certain to be complicated. On one hand, Avram said Israel would probably build him a new and finer house in return for his service to Kfar Shalom, but on the other hand there just might be a certain amount of awkwardness over the rather messy fate of the culprits, enemies though they were. No, there was no choice; he must stay with his village. And of course Zubaida was needed as well, to bring order from the chaos of bombed home and demoralized family . . .

But Zubaida failed to follow this reasoning. It never occurred to her not to go with her children.

"I shall send thee word and return when I can, oh my husband," she told Moussa with such staggering simplicity that protest died unborn. She had never in her life been further than three or four miles from Bab-il-Howa, yet she would go unquestioning into a new, strange, fearful world with her children. Moussa looked at her.

"Hayat will care for the household," he heard himself saying.

And then, just as the bearers moved gently down the hill with the stretchers, in the first faint light of the dawn, Jasmin fought off the morphine and roused herself for a last instant.

"Father?"

He took her fragile hand, and her fingers stirred in his. "You will come see us, Father?"

Moussa hesitated. Her question was in its way a symbol. The wall of his isolation was in much the same condition as the wall of his house. The new world would creep in, inevitable as the sea, and it would be his task to control and restrain, that it might be a beneficial trickle and not a destroying tidal wave. But there was no trying to keep it out altogether. Allah had made His will known.

The dark eyes were fixed on his, clouded but compelling.

"I shall come," he promised, and with the words he accepted Israel.

ARABIC GLOSSARY

aba: long, unseamed full outer robe

abou: father

Allah: God

Allah ysallmak: God makes all things easy.

Allaho akbar: God is great.

Bedouine: Bedouin girl; a wild, restless girl

Bismallah: In the name of Allah!

djinni: spirit (*djinn,* plural)

humus (or *choomus*): a dish of ground chick-peas and olive oil

ibn: son

Il hamdillah: Praise God.

Il mektub mektub: What is written is written.

imam: spiritual leader

ipe: shame; a shameful, disgraceful thing

jirdan: bedbug

kafer: village

kaftan: full belted women's robe

khaffiya: triangular headdress, held in place by rings of goat-hair cord, double, around crown of head

khamsin: hot wind from the desert

Koran: the scriptures of the Moslems

kus emmek: swearing

La Ilaha illa-Allah: There is no God but God (call to prayer).

mahr: bride-price, paid by bridegroom to bride's father

Mashallah: God wills it.

maskin: miserable specimen, wretch (not really translatable)

mausaf: a dish of meat, rice, sauce
mukhtar: village head
pita: flat, thin unleavened bread
purdah: the seclusion of women
Salaam: Peace (a greeting and farewell).
Salaam aleikum: Peace be with you (also greeting and
  farewell).
Shaitan: Satan
tob: long cotton garment reaching to ankles
Wallah!: exclamation, literally "Let's go!"
ya abou: my father
Yahudi: Jew (*Yahud,* plural)

HEBREW GLOSSARY

abba: father
ain devar: it's all right
ben: son
chaver: friend, pal, comrade (*chaverim,* plural)
eretz: land
kfar: village
khutzpah: cheeky, brash person
kibbutz: a community settlement
kibbutznik: someone who lives on a kibbutz
Knesset: Israel's equivalent of Congress or Parliament
Shalom: Peace (greeting or farewell)
Shalom aleichem: Peace be with you. Same as *Salaam
  aleikum.*
tov: good

SALLY WATSON comments, "I read omniverously as a child —everything except my school lessons. Read my way steadily through school, in fact, on library books hidden on my lap. But I managed to get my B.A. from Reed College in Portland, Oregon in spite—or because—of this . . ."

Now, Miss Watson is the author of many books for young readers including *Highland Rebel, Mistress Malapert, Lark* and *The Hornet's Nest,* historical novels sharing a family tree; and a group set in the Near East with many characters drawn from several families, *To Build a Land, Other Sandals,* and *The Mukhtar's Children.* She has traveled extensively in Europe and the Near East and gathered much of her background material for *The Mukhtar's Children* as well as her other books on location. She is also active in Mensa and the Royal Scottish Dance Society and has recently taken up Judo, being graded up to 4th Kyu (Orange Belt) after six months' training. Among her varied pleasures Miss Watson numbers Highland dancing, cats, fencing, BBC radio, and gardening around the cottage in the English countryside where she lives.